CUF

Please renew/return this item by the last date shown.
Please call the number below:

Renewals and enquiries: 0300 123 4049

Textphone for hearing or
speech impaired users: 0300 123 4041

www.hertsdirect.org/librarycatalogue

L32

Look out for more

stories!

Star Crossed
Strictly Friends?

Coming soon:

Ice Dreams
Model Behaviour

sweet
he♥rts

Forget Me Not

Jo Cotterill

RED FOX

SWEET HEARTS: FORGET ME NOT
A RED FOX BOOK 978 1 849 41217 9

First published in Great Britain by Red Fox Books,
an imprint of Random House Children's Books,
A Random House Group Company

This edition published 2011

1 3 5 7 9 10 8 6 4 2

The Random House Group Limited supports the Forest Stewardship
Council (FSC), the leading international forest certification organization.
All our titles that are printed on Greenpeace-approved FSC-certified paper
carry the FSC logo. Our paper procurement policy can be found at
www.randomhouse.co.uk/environment.

Mixed Sources
Product group from well-managed
forests and other controlled sources
www.fsc.org Cert no. TT-COC-002139
© 1996 Forest Stewardship Council

Red Fox Books are published by Random House Children's Books,
61–63 Uxbridge Road, London W5 5SA

www.**kids**at**randomhouse**.co.uk
www.**totallyrandombooks**.co.uk

Addresses for companies within The Random House Group Limited
can be found at: www.randomhouse.co.uk/offices.htm

THE RANDOM HOUSE GROUP Limited Reg. No. 954009

A CIP catalogue record for this book is available from the British Library.

Printed and bound in Great Britain by
CPI Bookmarque, Croydon, CR0 4TD

For my mum, who taught me everything
I needed to know about gardening.

And for Great-Uncle Johnny,
who taught her.

Chapter 1

Rosemary

The May sunlight filtered through the trees, making shifting dappled patterns on the grass. The day was warm with a light breeze, and Kate lifted her face to the sun, closing her eyes. There was such an ache in her heart it was hard to breathe.

Her grandfather, sitting beside her on the bench, patted her hand. 'I expect she's looking down on you right now and smiling.'

Kate drew her hand away. 'I'm not a child, Anpa. You can't know where she is, or even if she exists at all.'

'Sorry, love. I suppose you just say the things you think you ought to say without really thinking about them. But that doesn't mean there isn't a possibility . . . that she *is* looking down on you and smiling. She'd be proud of you. How much you've grown up in the last three years.'

'Three years . . .' Kate couldn't speak any more.

Three years to the day since her mother had died. Sometimes it felt so much longer than that; other times it felt as if it were only yesterday. All those visits to hospital, all that awful treatment, seeing Mum get weaker and weaker every day . . . it wasn't something you forgot easily. And every time this anniversary came round, it seemed to get harder, not easier. *Surely*, she thought, *people told me time was a healer?*

'It's not right,' Anpa said quietly. 'That's what you feel, isn't it? And I know what you mean. Cynthia was always so *alive*. Like all of this.' He waved a hand at the view before them. Trees glossy with leaves reached up to the blue sky, whilst narrow paths wound in and out of flower beds and through secluded shrub-beries bordered by forget-me-nots. 'All living and breathing.'

'It's not fair,' mumbled Kate. 'Why her?'

Her grandfather was silent.

Kate took another breath. She knew there was no point asking that kind of question; she'd asked it enough since her mother had died and there simply wasn't a good answer. But it didn't stop her trying to find one. 'Sorry,' she said quietly.

Anpa took her hand again. 'Never be sorry,' he told her. 'Your mother was a bright shining star. And we all miss her. You, me and your father.' His voice wobbled a little, but he cleared his throat. 'We'll never forget her. How could we, when everything she loved is all around us?'

Kate smiled despite herself. Anpa was right, of course. Her mother had loved flowers and nature. Suddenly three years felt like three minutes and she could almost see her mother running through the trees, smiling and waving at her; calling out, 'They've got three new rose varieties, come and see! The pink one is just beautiful; it would be perfect for wedding bouquets!' For Cynthia, a visit to the Botanic Gardens had always been a source of inspiration for her floristry creations. Even gazing up at a huge beech tree could give her an idea for a new table decoration or a 'room feature'. She'd started small, but within a few years had become one of the most sought-after florists in the country, able to charge enormous amounts of money to provide flower designs for weddings or corporate events.

Kate's hand went automatically to her lap, where there lay a small bunch of rosemary, tied with a white ribbon. *Rosemary for remembrance* went the saying, and Kate knew her mother had used it in many bridal bouquets over the years 'to remember those who are no longer with us'. They had a large rosemary bush at home and Kate always brought a sprig when she visited the Botanics now.

'You going to leave that here on the bench?' Anpa asked, noticing the gesture.

'Yes.'

Anpa nodded. 'She didn't sit still much, our Cynthia, but she did like the view from this bench.'

The two of them looked around. Unknown to the staff at the Botanics, Kate, Anpa and Kate's father Nick had scattered Cynthia's ashes right here across the perfectly manicured lawns. Nick had been quite sure there would be no point asking for permission: 'It's a public place – they couldn't say yes to us in case everyone starts doing it.'

Anpa had shrugged and said, 'It was my daughter's favourite place in the world. If they won't give permission, then we won't ask for it.'

So they had taken the ashes in a Tupperware container ('That urn is too obvious,' said Anpa, 'and Cynthia wasn't proud') and carried it right into the heart of the gardens, where the three of them sat down on a bench and waited until there were no people in sight. Then Nick had got up, wiping his eyes, and opened the lid of the container. There wasn't a breath of movement in the air, but just as the tub was opened, a sudden gust blew up out of nowhere and suddenly the air was full of Cynthia's ashes. Kate had stared up in astonishment: in the sunlight, it seemed as though the air were full of tiny fireflies, twisting and dancing.

Kate treasured that moment. At night, when she was in bed and the loneliness seemed too much to bear, she unwrapped the memory like a gift. The image of the tiny flickering specks of light comforted her. She imagined that her mother, so vibrant in life, had been transported into some kind of elemental form. 'Ashes to ashes,' the prayer went: 'dust to dust' – but what dust! Sparkling, effervescent bubbles of light – wonderful! That memory almost erased those other, more painful memories. Almost.

Kate jumped slightly as Anpa squeezed her arm. 'You see that oak? Two hundred years old, it is.'

Kate smiled. She knew exactly what Anpa was going to say because he said it every single time they came. 'Older than you, older than me . . .' she joined in.

Anpa laughed. 'Said it before, haven't I? Well, it's still true though. Older than you, older than me, it'll be here long after we've gone. To that tree, we're just the blink of an eye.' He snapped his fingers. 'Here today, gone tomorrow, like *that*.'

'Anpa, is that supposed to make me feel better?'

'Of course! How could it not cheer you up, know-ing that?' Anpa gestured towards the tree. 'Because it doesn't matter how long you're here for, pet, it only matters what you *do* with your time.'

'What has the tree done then?'

'Given pleasure to hundreds and thousands of people,' said Anpa simply. 'Look at it. What a thing of beauty! Now, your mother . . .' Kate felt a pang as he said the word. 'She may only have been thirty-eight,' went on Anpa, 'but what thirty-eight years! Full of love and laughter and beauty. She brought happiness to so many people through her work. Remember how many letters she'd get, thanking her for making the wedding day so perfect? She made people happy. *That's* what matters.'

Kate felt her mouth tremble slightly. She wondered sadly if *she* had that effect on anyone. *I can barely remember what it was like to be properly, completely happy*, she thought. *If I were to die, would I have done anything that mattered? Would I have made a differ-ence to anyone?*

Anpa, following his own train of thought, sighed. 'It's a shame your father couldn't come. We should all be together on a day like this.'

'He said he'd come this evening, after work.' Kate stared at the tree again. 'You know he still comes here

6

at night. Eleven o'clock and sometimes even later. He climbs over the fence.'

Anpa shook his head. 'It's not right to grieve alone. He should come with us.'

Kate said nothing. She could understand how her father felt. Sharing the tears didn't make them go away.

Anpa got to his feet. 'Come on, pet. My knees are seizing up, I need a walk.'

Kate carefully laid the bunch of rosemary on the bench. 'I miss you,' she whispered. Then she stood up and tucked her hand through the crook of Anpa's arm.

'Let's go down to the water garden,' Anpa suggested. 'See if the red lotus is out yet.'

'All right. I can take a photo for Dad. He likes water lilies.'

'He works too many hours,' Anpa said, frowning. 'Why couldn't he take a day off to come? Compassionate leave or something? Surely there can't be so much to do that they couldn't spare him?'

'He said things are really busy at the office right now.'

Nick worked for a large furnishing company as Head of European Sales. His wife had been a high earner and had left some money in a trust for Kate when she reached eighteen. Nick was determined to keep the family 'comfortable,' as he called it, though Kate wondered uneasily why he seemed to be home so rarely these days. Even hard workers had days off, didn't they? Whereas her father seemed to spend all his time in the office.

Anpa read her mind. 'All work and no play makes people dull. Your father should find time for you.'

Kate squeezed his hand. 'I don't mind. I get to spend time with you instead.'

Her grandfather smiled at her. 'We rub along all right, don't we? And it's companionable in the garden.' His look became mischievous. 'As long as you don't boss me around too much.'

Kate's jaw dropped. '*Me* boss *you* around?' Then she saw he was joking. 'I think we both know who's in charge of our garden. Since you moved in, it's changed completely.'

'No use wasting space if it could feed us,' said Anpa smugly. 'All those flowers Cynthia grew – very pretty but no good for supper. Which reminds me, I was wondering about a cherry tree this year . . .'

'No, Anpa,' said Kate firmly. 'There's definitely no more room for trees, you know there isn't.'

'But if we took out the tulips . . .'

'I *like* the tulips.'

'You can't eat them,' complained Anpa. 'You like all the useless plants!'

'Just because they're pretty . . .' began Kate hotly, and then she caught her grandfather's eye and realized he was teasing again. 'Don't do that, Anpa. You know I love the flowers.' *They remind me of Mum.*

'I know, petal.' He squeezed her hand. 'Just trying to make you smile. Not an easy task, these days.'

Kate bit her lip. She knew that something in her had changed when her mother died. How could it not? The world was different and she felt as though she herself would never be the same again. The sun still shone but it didn't make her happy. Time ticked away but she no longer looked forward to things. Only flowers seemed to have any kind of meaning now, because they brought her closer to her mum's memory. *And why didn't I care about the flowers before she died?* Kate wondered. *Why didn't I try to share in something that she loved so much before it was too late?*

'Oh.' She stopped in disappointment as they reached the water garden. 'The red lotuses aren't out yet.'

'Yes, they are.' Anpa pointed to a shady corner of the pool. 'There's one single bloom over there, look.'

Kate pulled out her phone to take a picture. 'If

Dad comes later, it'll be all closed up.' She wondered briefly if the rosemary would still be on the bench by then or whether some officious gardener would have cleared it away and put it on the compost heap. Her eyes stung suddenly and she had to take three photos on the phone before she got one that wasn't blurry from her shaking hand.

'We should be getting home,' commented Anpa, his sharp gaze missing nothing. 'Good weather today, lots to do in the garden; we should make the most of it.'

Kate was reluctant. 'Can't we stay a bit longer?'

He looked at her sympathetically. 'We've been here long enough, pet. Can't spend all day moping. Keeping busy, that's the best thing. Now, about the summer fruits. I think we'll need to get some more netting. Last year the birds ate half the raspberries and I'm not having that happen again.'

Kate nodded absently.

'I'll get some at Tilworths next week,' Anpa went on cheerfully. 'They've got good strong stuff and it's not too expensive. Though I've told Mike a hundred times he should get in some black netting as well as the green. It lasts longer in the sunlight. But he just says, "Yes, John, I quite agree," and does nothing about it! Probably thinks I'm interfering as usual.' He grinned suddenly. 'They must be sick of the sight of me by now.'

Kate smiled at last. 'I don't think so. You're their best customer!' Her forehead furrowed again. 'I was wondering, Anpa . . . do you think I could get a summer job this year?'

Her grandfather stopped so suddenly that she'd taken several paces before she realized he was no longer with her. 'Don't you dare,' he said sternly. 'You're too young, you don't want to even be thinking about that kind of thing.'

'I'm not too young, Anpa. There *are* jobs for people my age, you know. Paper rounds and supermarkets and things.'

He looked curiously at her. 'Why do you want one?'

'I'd like to keep busy.' She pushed back some curls of hair. 'And we're not going anywhere on holiday.'

Anpa sighed. 'I know. Your father's work again.'

'So there'll be six weeks to fill. Megan's going abroad for half the time, and I'd like something to do.'

'What about helping me in the garden?'

Kate sighed impatiently. 'I do that anyway, Anpa. I don't want to be stuck at home all day getting bored.' Immediately the words were out, she regretted them. He looked hurt. 'Not that I mean being with you is boring, Anpa.'

'I'm not stopping you from going out, Kate. I'd *like* you to go out more – so would your father. It's just that you never seem to want to.'

'Well, now I do. I want a job.' *Like other people*, she thought. *I want to be normal, more like I used to be. Not trapped inside this little box of grief, the box labelled 'Motherless'.*

'All right then.' Anpa took a breath. 'I suppose it might be nice for you to earn a bit of your own money too. You could buy something nice for yourself. What do you want to do?'

'I'm not sure. I was wondering – do you think I could work here?' She looked around hopefully. 'I know quite a lot about flowers now.'

Her grandfather hesitated. 'I don't suppose the Botanics would hire you, love. Worth asking, but they probably have all the gardeners they need. Somewhere smaller, that might do you. Like a garden centre or a nursery. You could do worse than Tilworths, of course. Why don't I have a word with Janet and Mike?'

'Would you?' Kate felt a rush of affection. Anpa had moved in just after her mother's death and had been her rock, propping her up and encouraging her through every difficult day since. She spent more time with him than her own father now.

'Of course. Like you say, I'm their best customer. I'm sure they'd take my granddaughter for a summer job. Why don't we head over there now?' His eyes gleamed. 'And while we're there, we could pick up a few things . . .'

Chapter 2

Heather

'Here you go.' Janet Tilworth handed over a large green apron with TILWORTHS embroidered on the top. Kate slipped it over her head. 'You'll need to tie it up quite tightly,' commented Janet, her eyes crinkling at the corners. 'It's a bit big for you. More suited to someone a little taller, I'm afraid.'

Kate fumbled with the ties, catching her curly brown hair in the knot by mistake. She didn't know why she was nervous. She had been to Tilworths garden centre plenty of times with Anpa over the last couple of years. Janet and Mike Tilworth were always friendly and kind to her as a customer – but working for them was another matter. Kate hoped that she would do everything right first time and not mess up.

'Now, I'm sure you already know where everything is.' Janet smiled and glanced at her husband Mike, a tall man with beefy arms and a sunburned face. 'Your granddad brings you here often enough.'

Mike chuckled. 'Knows his stuff, he does. And never short of an opinion either.' Then he saw that Kate was embarrassed. 'Bless you, we don't mind. If we had a pound for each time we'd been criticized, well . . .'

'We'd be retired and living in Mauritius,' finished Janet with a snort.

'Exactly. We're thick-skinned,' Mike told Kate. 'Got to be in this business. And at least your granddad knows what he's talking about, unlike *some* people.' Janet gave another snort. 'Anyway, we can't stand around here all morning,' Mike went on hastily. 'We need to show you what you'll be doing.'

Tilworths garden centre wasn't big, but it certainly made use of all available space. The entrance to the centre was through the main shop, which sold bird feeders, seeds, bulbs, lawn feed and other small items in boxes. To the right of the entrance were the two tills, and to the left, the building extended round the corner in an 'L' shape. In the furthest part of the shop were the flower-arranging items; there was also a stand of scented candles, several racks of greetings cards and notepads and pens, a tool area and a large section for garden furniture. At the very end of the shop there was a staff door with an electronic code and it was through this that Mike and Janet took Kate.

'The code for the door is twelve-thirty,' Mike told Kate in a low voice. He grinned. 'Lunch time, that's how I remember it.'

'Toilet's right in front of you,' Janet pointed out. 'And then just through here to the left is the staff room. Well, I say staff room – you can leave your bag in here and eat lunch, but there's not much space.'

Kate looked around. The 'staff room' was cramped, with three low uncomfortable-looking armchairs and a small square window. Shelves lined the walls and there were also two filing cabinets, one of which looked as though it had seen better days. The top drawer stuck out an inch or so and Kate could see this was because it was stuffed full of paper.

'Invoices and receipts,' Janet told her. 'We have to keep everything for six years for the tax office. Though in fact I'm not sure we've ever emptied the cabinets; we just seem to put more in. Maybe if you've got time over the summer, you could go through some of it and throw out the stuff that's twenty years out of date.' She pointed to a white board near the window. 'That's the "to do" list – we try to keep it as up-to-date as possible. Wipe off a job once you've done it, otherwise someone else might be sent to do it a second time.'

Kate peered at the scrawls on the board and could just make out: *Check ceramic pots for chips and discount if nec, Move gargoyles to gravel area, Clean fountains* and things like that. She was pleased to find that she understood all the jobs on the list and knew she'd be able to do them if asked. The nervous part of her relaxed a little and she felt a bit excited at being allowed to see behind the scenes of the centre.

'Don't worry about these now,' said Mike, referring to the long list. 'We allocate jobs as and when they become priority. You'll get to do some of them. You and Simon.'

'Simon's starting tomorrow,' added Janet. 'He's on a summer job too.'

'Oh, right,' said Kate, wondering if she knew him. There was a Simon in her year at school, though she normally saw him playing football and couldn't imagine him working in a garden centre.

Janet glanced at her husband. 'We don't usually take on extra staff for the summer but our daughter Louise is off travelling and so we're a pair of hands down during the school holidays.'

'I'm very grateful,' said Kate hastily.

Janet laughed. 'Don't be. We're not doing you a favour; you'll have to work hard.'

Kate nodded. 'I'm used to that.'

'Your granddad orders you around in the garden, does he?' asked Mike with a twinkle in his eye.

'Definitely,' replied Kate with feeling, and the other two laughed.

'Come on,' said Janet. 'I'll take you round the rest. Mike needs to get back to work.'

'How many people work here?' asked Kate as they headed back out into the shop.

'There's me and Mike, Louise when she's not away, Jason who does the heavy lifting and Carol in the gift shop. Then in the nursery we also have Polly and Bob.'

Kate tried to remember all the names. She was sure she'd already met Carol in the shop, but the others were unfamiliar. Tilworths had its own nursery behind the garden centre; a large walled garden filled with rows and rows of greenhouses. It was where plants were grown from seed and kept before they were big enough to be sold in the centre.

'I'll show you round the nursery later,' said Janet. 'It's lovely in there, quite a different atmosphere to the centre, even though it's right next door. I expect Polly and Bob will be glad to have an extra pair of hands. There's always lots to do.'

They had reached the front of the shop now and Janet led the way through the covered walkway, past the hot house and out to the main display area. Garden ornaments jostled for space with climber frames and different-coloured gravel. Then there were the rows and rows of plants: tiny rock plants with silvery-grey leaves and miniature white flowers; big blowsy roses; tall slender delphiniums in deepest blue. Kate loved to walk up and down the shelves when she came with Anpa, drinking in the variety and colour on display.

Janet saw her face. 'I'm guessing this is your favourite part.'

Kate nodded. 'Anpa's always telling me to hurry up. He doesn't bother much with flowers.'

'Your mum was a florist, wasn't she?' asked Janet. 'I guess you take after her.' She smiled.

Kate ignored the twinge of pain she got whenever her mother was mentioned. 'Maybe, but I didn't really get interested until afterwards.'

'She was a genius with flowers,' Janet commented, a wistful look on her face. 'Mike ordered a bouquet from her once, for our anniversary. Absolutely stunning, it was. And it had some special message because of the flowers she used.'

'Yeah, she was really into flower meanings. She had all these books about the language of flowers. She'd design whole events around the meanings of three or four flowers. Like love and friendship, things like that. I've started reading them.'

Janet looked at her thoughtfully. 'Maybe you'll be a florist too?'

Kate shrugged. 'Not sure.' *I couldn't be anything like as good as she was. Mum was clever, really clever. Not just with flowers, but with her mind too. She was always top of the class at school, Anpa said. I wish I took after her more.*

'I'm sure your mum would have loved that,' said Janet. 'She was very cheerful and lively, everyone always said.'

Kate looked down. Her mother *had* been cheerful and lively, before her illness; she had been the energy at the centre of the family. And she had made everyone around her cheerful too. No wonder they didn't laugh so much in Kate's house now that the light at the centre had gone out.

'OK, must get on,' Janet said briskly, gesturing to her right. 'That's where the hoses and taps are. One of your jobs will be the daily watering. Make sure you bring wellies with you tomorrow so you don't get too wet.'

Kate relaxed a little as Janet continued to show her around, pointing out the areas she would be most likely to work in. 'Don't you usually have hanging baskets?' she asked as she looked up to the roof of the covered area.

'All sold by the beginning of June,' replied Janet. 'We keep baskets and matting out for sale but we don't plant up any more. People are more interested in vegetables and herbs during the summer. Salad stuff too.'

'What happened to that bit?' Kate pointed to a hole in the corner of the roof. The plastic had torn away from the jagged edge.

Janet pulled a face. 'Someone threw a rock through it a week or so ago.'

'A rock?' Kate stared. 'On purpose? Why?'

'Don't know. Kids, probably, having a laugh. We've had a few little bits of vandalism over the past few weeks.' Janet laughed but it didn't sound like she thought it was funny. 'They'll get bored soon, I expect. Nothing to worry about.' She shook herself, as though trying to get rid of a bad memory. 'I'm going to put you to work. Bob brought round a load of lilies earlier ready for sale. I need you to check them for lily beetles. Do you know what they look like?'

'Yes, I . . .' Kate's heart thumped. Why did her first

job have to be checking her mother's favourite plants? *Everyone loves lilies*, Cynthia would say, laughing. *'Lily' means beauty and elegance. Who doesn't want that at their wedding? I had lilies at my own wedding!* 'Small and bright red.'

'Good girl. Absolute scourge, they are. Make sure you check them really thoroughly. Then I want you to price them up. Hang on . . .' Janet dug a crumpled list out of her pocket. 'This is the list of varieties and their prices. You'll need to get the pricing gun from the staff room and ask Carol to show you how to use it. Put the prices on the labels rather than the pots, then they don't peel off so easily. When you've done all of those, go and tell Jason so that he can take them round to the right section and put them out on the shelves. Got that?'

Kate nodded.

'By the time you've done all of that, it'll probably be lunch time. Come and find me when you've finished here, OK?' Janet smiled and left.

Kate took a deep breath and turned to the pots of lilies. A sudden memory flashed across her vision: her mother, kneeling in the garden, carefully turning over leaf after leaf. *Not too fast*, she told a watching Kate, *in case they drop off the leaves and hide on the ground*. It had been a warm day, Kate remembered now, and her mother had been wearing a green cotton dress. Had she stayed to watch? She thought now that she'd probably gone off to play.

Kate dragged her brain back to the present. She mustn't stand around day-dreaming; she had a job to do. She needed to check for black eggs too, which would hatch into new beetles and destroy the plant. It was a laborious task but Kate was determined to do it properly. She needed to prove to Janet and Mike that they had done the right thing by hiring her.

She just wished she could have avoided the lilies for the first day at least.

♥

'And what did you do after that?' asked Kate's father Nick, in between mouthfuls of fish fingers, new potatoes and salad.

'Had lunch in the staff room,' said Kate. 'Well, I started off in there, but it got really hot, so Janet opened the fire door for me. There's a little area out there in between the sheds where they put stuff that doesn't belong anywhere else.'

'I hope they looked after you,' commented Nick.

'I don't need looking after, Dad. I'm there to work.'

'I know, but you're still a child.' Her father smiled at her.

Kate felt a stab of irritation. 'I'm not a child.'

'Anyway,' Anpa put in hastily, 'go on, love. What did you do in the afternoon?'

'Helped to clear the shelves,' Kate replied, still annoyed with her father. 'You know, when people take the plant pot from the back of the row rather than the front – everything just needs tidying up, that's all. And removing dead leaves or branches from plants that have got bumped, so that they don't put people off. And after that, I helped Janet re-organize the ceramic pots because they're not selling very well and she thought the display wasn't very good.'

'Sounds like you've had a full day.' Anpa patted her arm. 'You should make sure you have an early night. How about hot chocolate in front of the TV this evening?' He turned to Kate's father. 'Why don't we all do that?'

Nick shook his head. 'Sorry. I've got to go back to the office.'

There was a little pause. Kate bit her lip.

'Again?' asked Anpa. Kate could tell he wasn't impressed. 'What could possibly need doing this evening?'

'Accounts,' said Nick. 'Paperwork. Emails.'

'Can't you do them tomorrow?'

Nick avoided his gaze. 'No. If I don't do them tonight, they won't get done. I've got back-to-back meetings tomorrow.'

'Do you have to go back to the office, though? Can't you do them here on the laptop?'

'I need access to the files.' Nick shrugged, sounding impatient. 'All the paperwork is there.'

Anpa sighed.

Kate placed her knife and fork onto her plate as silently as she could.

Her father ran his hand through his hair. 'Look, I'm sorry things are so frantic at the moment. They'll calm down in a couple of weeks when we've got the sales conference out of the way.'

Kate nodded, though she didn't believe him. Her father had become a workaholic ever since her mother had died. She didn't think things would change in a few weeks' time.

Nick smiled at his daughter. 'I'm sorry, love. You can tell me more about it tomorrow. The important thing is that you enjoyed yourself.'

'I did.' And she meant it. 'I liked being out in the fresh air all day, and it's kind of a nice atmosphere. Everyone just lets me get on with things. There's someone else coming for summer work tomorrow

too. A boy, about my age. I think he might be someone from school.'

Anpa brightened up. 'That'll be nice for you, to
have someone else your age to talk to. You spend too
much time with old fuddy-duddies like me.'

'You're not a fuddy-duddy, Anpa,' Kate said,
amused.

'Yes, I am. You should be spending more time with
friends of your own age. Back before . . .' He hesitated. 'You know, *before*, you used to have lots of
friends. I remember you were always round someone else's house. What was that girl's name? Tammy?
Tara?'

'Tasha.'

'Tasha, that's right. Always talking about her, you
were. And the other girls in that group. I know you
had a bit of a falling out or something, but surely
that's all water under the bridge now, isn't it? Can't
you meet up with them?'

Kate felt her face redden. 'N-no. Not really. We –
don't talk much nowadays.'

'I think that's a shame,' Anpa pursued the point.
'You used to get on so well, always having dress-up
parties and making cakes together. Why don't you
give her a call sometime?'

'No,' said Kate miserably, 'I can't.'

Her father came unexpectedly to her rescue. 'Leave her alone, John. She doesn't want to talk about it.'

Anpa sighed. 'I just don't like to see her on her own all the time,' he said.

Kate felt like curling up into a ball. Her grandfather was right, of course. She did have a circle of friends, before . . . before her mother died. And Tasha, of course. Tasha had been her best friend for ages. But then it had all gone wrong, and now it was far too late to pick up from three years ago. 'I have Megan,' she said, with a spark of rebellion. She'd met Megan in the school canteen before Christmas and instantly found her easy to talk to.

Anpa nodded slowly. 'That's true. She seems nice. I'm glad you met her. All that dancing though, she's so busy. And it's not as though you've known her for very long.'

Nick wiped his plate clean with a piece of bread and made his voice more cheerful. 'Is she coming round in the holidays? You should ask her. Maybe the two of you could go to the cinema or something.'

Kate shook her head. 'She's off on holiday next week, for three weeks, remember?'

'Sorry, love, I'd forgotten. Where's she going?'

'Cyprus,' said Kate. 'With Jake and his family. I mean, they're all going together. It's a self-catering

place with a pool.' She tried to ignore a jealous pang
somewhere in her stomach region. Back when her
mother was alive, they'd had holidays like that too
– extravagant weeks in Tunisia, Rome, Brittany. But
they hadn't been on holiday for three years now. It
wasn't the money, Kate knew. It was just that her
father made excuse after excuse – there was too much
on at work, they'd go next year, he couldn't be away
just now. *I wish Megan had asked me to go with them*,
a small voice whispered inside Kate's head, but as
Anpa had pointed out, she and Megan had only been
friends for a matter of months, whereas Jake's family
had lived next door to Megan's for years. And there
was the extra matter of Megan and Jake being an item
too, of course. Megan always tried to include her, but
Kate felt like a gooseberry when Jake was around.

'I went to Cyprus once,' Nick commented, 'with a
group of lads.'

'What was it like?'

Her dad wiped his mouth and pushed back his
chair. 'To be honest, I can't remember much about
it. There was a lot of drinking and falling over.' He
screwed up his face in an effort of concentration. 'I'm
trying to remember if there was anything else . . . but
no. Drinking and falling over.'

Kate was unimpressed. 'Doesn't sound very exciting.' In fact, it sounded like some of the parties her friends had talked about at school recently – her ex-friends, that is. Kate hadn't been invited, of course, and although she didn't really think she would have enjoyed it, it would have been nice to be asked.

Nick grinned at her affectionately. 'It wasn't. But at the time it seemed like a really good idea.' He glanced at the clock. 'Got to go. I've got a mountain of paper-work to get through. Don't stay up too late.'

'Yeah, yeah.' Kate thought it was a bit rich, her father telling her not to stay up late when he himself didn't come home from work until midnight, but she said nothing. She knew Anpa was thinking the same thing by the way he clicked his tongue against his teeth.

Nick kissed his daughter on the head and grabbed his coat and keys, banging the door behind him.

Anpa opened his mouth.

'Don't say it.'

Anpa shrugged. 'Yet again, he's off to work when he should be here with you. It's like he doesn't . . .' He trailed off and gave Kate a half-hearted smile. 'Never mind. I'll clear away, love, you go and have a sit down.'

Kate finished the sentence in her own head as she headed to the sitting-room sofa. *It's like he doesn't care about us any more. Even his own daughter.* She wanted to believe it wasn't true, but it was hard when Dad only seemed to come home to eat, never to spend an evening with her. *Doesn't he like me any more?* she wondered miserably.

As she sat down on the sofa, another memory thudded into her mind. It seemed to be happening more and more often these days – remembering how life used to be, before.

'Come on, Kate!' a girl with a long blonde ponytail yelled. Tasha. 'Bring your big feet over here! The roller-coaster's this way!'

Kate grinned, excitement filling her lungs along with the warm summer air. 'You said you wouldn't dare!'

'I will if you will!'

The rollercoaster was enormous; yellow track snaking round and round and up into the sky. 'Are we tall enough?' Tasha asked. 'They might not let us on.'

Kate stuck out her tongue. 'You scared?'

'No!' said Tasha defensively. 'Just saying.'

'We're fine – look.' Kate stood next to the height chart at the start of the queue. 'Come on.'

By the time they reached the front of the queue, Tasha was shaking. 'It's so fast,' she gulped. 'And that bit where it goes round the corkscrew – I'm not sure, Kate . . .'

Kate grinned at her friend. 'Are you kidding? It looks awesome! You'll love it when we're on it, bet you anything.'

'Next group,' said the bored ride assistant, opening the gates to let them through. Kate ran straight for the front car.

'Not the front!' groaned Tasha. 'I'll be sick!'

'Oh, don't be stupid. Here, give me your hand.'

The padded bars came down over their heads, and Tasha whimpered. 'I want to get off.'

'Too late now,' said Kate, her body fizzing with excitement as the car started the long, clacking ascent to the top of the first hill. The world dropped dizzyingly away as they climbed higher and higher. Then everything paused for a moment, and Kate and Tasha could see the long winding track dipping below them. Kate glanced at her friend to see her eyes closed tightly, and she smiled again. 'You're missing the view—' she started to say, but at that moment the car began its hurtling descent, and her breath was whipped away by the wind. Kate screamed in delight as the coaster whirled her round and round and upside down.

All too soon it was over, and the bars were lifting over their heads. Kate looked at Tasha. 'That was amazing!'

Tasha, slightly green, smiled shakily back. 'Actually, it wasn't as bad as I thought.'

'Told you.' They climbed out of the cars and headed for the exit.

Tasha hesitated. 'Do you think . . .'

'What?'

'Could we go on it again? It's just that I had my eyes closed for half of it.'

Kate beamed. 'Course. We'll have to queue again.'

'I don't mind.' Tasha smiled at her friend. 'I'd never have dared go on it if you hadn't made me.'

'I didn't make you . . .'

'But it was really cool.' Tasha shook her head. 'You're such a daredevil, Kate!'

Kate laughed. No one had ever called her a daredevil before and she liked it. 'I am a bit! Come on then, let's go round again!'

Kate stared at the patterned carpet now. How long ago had it been? It was a school trip, she knew that. They must have been about ten years old. The memory was so vivid and yet Kate felt as though her mind was somehow playing tricks on her. She couldn't remember how she felt in those days. A dare-devil? That can't have been her, surely. She must have remembered it wrong.

But Tasha had always looked to Kate for guidance, for a helping hand, encouragement. Kate had been the strong one, hadn't she? The leader, in a way, making decisions for the two of them. Others had followed too, and Kate was looked to for crazy, fun ideas.

And then her mum died. And somehow there wasn't any more crazy and fun. There was only darkness and tears. And Tasha, once Kate's faithful friend, began to tire of this new, quiet Kate. 'Why can't you just cheer up a bit?' she would whine. 'You can't be depressed *all* the time.'

But you can be, Kate thought. *You really can*. And so she had got cross with Tasha, telling her she didn't understand, to leave her alone. And eventually Tasha had indeed left Kate alone and gone off with other, newer, more exciting friends. And by the time Kate realized she minded, it was too late.

'I brought you a hot chocolate.' Anpa came in with a steaming mug.

'Thanks, Anpa.'

'You look shattered, love. Why don't you go to bed?'

'Yeah. Yeah, I think I will.' Kate got off the sofa and kissed her grandfather. 'Night, Anpa.'

'Night, love.'

As Kate climbed the stairs wearily, the mug clasped in her hand, she wished Anpa hadn't reminded her of Tasha, and of her old life. There was Megan now, thank goodness, and it was nice to have someone to sit with at lunch again, but Megan had Jake as her best friend. She couldn't be Kate's best friend as well. It was a bit sad that Kate's closest friend was her grandfather. But she'd pushed everyone else away, hadn't she?

Chapter 3

Fig

'Kate!' Janet called. 'Come over here a minute.'

Kate put down the pricing gun and wiped her hands on her apron.

Standing with Janet was a tall boy with black hair and tanned skin. 'This is Simon,' Janet told Kate. 'He'll be working the same days as you over the summer. Polly says they need some help potting up in the nursery. Can you two handle it?'

Kate glanced at Simon. He definitely wasn't the Simon she knew from school. She was sure she'd never seen him before. His dark eyes met hers briefly before he looked away and out across the rows of plants. She felt faintly offended – it was almost as though he hadn't seen her at all. 'Uh – yeah, of course. I haven't finished pricing these herbs yet though.'

'That doesn't matter, you can do them this

afternoon. You remember where all the potting-up stuff is, right?'

'Yes.'

'Great. So if you could take Simon round and show him where everything is . . .'

'OK. Um.' Kate bit her lip and said hesitantly to Simon, 'If you come with me . . .'

He nodded brusquely and followed her through the display area to the nursery gate. Kate felt more than a little uncomfortable. She didn't talk to boys at school much, and this one looked very unapproachable. She cast around in her mind for something to say. 'Um . . . do you come here a lot?' *Great! What a stupid question!*

Simon shrugged. 'A bit.'

'Oh. I – haven't seen you around.' *Now it sounds like I live here or something!*

Simon rolled his eyes. 'Where's this potting-up stuff then?'

Kate's face was hot with embarrassment. 'This way,' she said, hoping she sounded confident.

At the end of a large greenhouse was a high bench covered in pots and compost. There was also a trolley laden with several shelves of seedling trays. Green shoots were bursting over the edges. 'I guess these are the plants to be potted up,' commented Kate.

'You think?' said Simon in a sarcastic tone. 'What are they?' He reached past Kate, who was scarlet again, and pulled out the white identity peg. 'Aquilegia.'

'Also known as columbine,' Kate blurted out. She didn't know why but she suddenly had an irresistible urge to impress this boy; he seemed so superior. 'Columbine means *folly*, like foolishness, in the language of flowers. And aquilegia means *modesty*, which is a bit strange because they're the same plant. Though you can get different varieties, double-headed and variegated. We've got some purple ones in our garden: they mean *Resolved to win*, which is kind of funny really.'

Simon stared at her, his dark eyes unamused. 'Why is it funny?'

Kate floundered. 'Er – well, you know, it's just a bit . . . um . . .' She trailed off, her face burning. *Why on earth did you even open your mouth?*

'Aquilegia is poisonous,' Simon stated flatly.

Kate frowned. 'Poisonous? No it's not, it grows wild everywhere . . .'

'Poisonous,' repeated Simon matter-of-factly. 'If you eat the roots and seeds.'

Kate tried to laugh. 'I don't believe you. What kind of poisonous?'

'You get sick. And it can be fatal.'

'You can *die* from eating them?' Kate was astonished. 'No – you must have got it wrong. I never heard that.'

Simon shrugged. 'Maybe you don't know everything.'

Kate bit her tongue. Somewhere deep inside was a tiny spark of rebellion. The old Kate would have challenged Simon; shown him what she thought of his patronizing tone. But the new Kate was too used to keeping her head down, not getting involved. It was easier that way.

Simon took one of the trays off the shelf. 'We'd better get on with this. You prepare the new trays and I'll push out the plug plants.'

Before she knew what she was doing, Kate had half filled one of the trays with compost. Then her brain kicked in. Simon had taken charge, just like that! And she had actually *followed orders*! The spark inside her flickered again. *What an arrogant boy!* she thought angrily to herself. How dare he come in on his first day and start telling her what to do!

'You done that one yet?' Simon glanced across. 'Let's have it then.'

Kate shoved it along the bench, spilling some of the compost as she did, but Simon made no comment. Instead, he expertly pinched the bottom of

each plug plant to release it from its tiny compart-
ment before easing it out, dipping a finger into the
new soil and carefully placing the seedling in its new
home. Kate's jaw dropped. He had clearly done this
before; there was no hesitation in his fingers. In fact,
he looked as though he'd been doing it all his life.
Even *more* annoying!

Simon saw her staring and said bluntly, 'What?'

'Nothing.' Kate couldn't believe it. Her lovely
summer job at Tilworths looked like it was going to
be ruined by this new boy. Yesterday she'd been in
oasis of calm, surrounded by beautiful flowers and
left to carry out her jobs alone. Simon had only been
here half an hour and already the day was spoiled.
He might be a natural gardener but he was also an
annoying know-it-all! She just *knew* he was going to
put her down all the time.

Kate glared at her trays of compost as they worked
silently. She wished Simon had never come!

♥

When Polly came to find them two hours later, she
was pleasantly surprised. 'You *have* been working
well!' she exclaimed. 'I can't believe the progress you've
made. We'll have them done in no time.'

Kate was pleased that Polly was happy, but it had been an awful morning as far as she was concerned. And they hadn't even finished potting up all the plants! She dreaded the thought of working all day with Simon.

'Why don't you two go off and have lunch?' suggested Polly. 'You deserve a break, and it's twelve o'clock.'

'I don't mind staying and doing some more,' Kate said hopefully, 'whilst Simon has his lunch. Then we could swap.'

'No, no,' said Polly, 'you both go off together. It's nice to have some company, isn't it?'

No, thought Kate, but she didn't want to offend Polly.

They washed the worst of the dirt off their hands at an outside tap, the cold water making Kate's fingers tingle. Then they headed back to the main building, Simon punching in the code to allow them into the staff area. Kate went straight to her bag to dig out her packed lunch. Simon gave her cling-film-wrapped sandwiches a disparaging look. 'They're cheese and pickle,' Kate felt obliged to say and was then cross with herself for being so defensive. What business of his was it if she had cheese and pickle sandwiches? Honestly!

Simon picked up a plastic bag and looked around. 'Are we supposed to eat in here?'

'We don't have to. There's a place to sit outside.' Kate pushed open the fire door. 'Out here.'

Simon looked critically at the little yard, dotted with broken and no-longer-for-sale objects. 'It's not much.'

'At least it's out in the fresh air.' She stepped onto the cracked paving.

Simon shrugged. 'True. Better than that stuffy room anyway.'

Is he going to complain all day? Kate fumed to herself. She sat down on a split wooden toadstool and unwrapped her sandwiches, determined not to start any more conversations. She hadn't realized how hungry she was, and she'd devoured one and a half sandwiches before she noticed what Simon was eating. From a small Tupperware pot he'd taken out what looked like a green sausage – it couldn't be, could it? No, it wasn't a sausage – was it made of *leaves*?

Kate tried not to stare, but she couldn't for the life of her imagine what it might be. Once Simon had eaten his green leaf sausage, he pulled out another pot and a spoon and started to eat the contents. *Now this I recognize*, Kate thought to herself. *It's couscous. But it's got bits in it – red bits and green bits and white bits*. A faint scent of sundried tomatoes reached her nose. It smelled delicious.

Kate glanced down at her cheese-and-pickle sandwich. Suddenly it didn't look so appetizing. She felt unreasonably cross. Why hadn't he brought sandwiches like a *normal* person? Now he'd spoiled her *lunch* as well as her morning!

'Janet said your grandfather comes here a lot,' Simon announced out of the blue. 'She said he likes bossing them about.'

Kate felt her hackles rise. 'He doesn't boss them about,' she snapped back. 'He just knows a lot about gardening, that's all.' *And I bet that's not what Janet said*.

'Like you?' Simon raised his eyebrows.

'I never said I know a lot about gardening,' said Kate, rising to the bait even though she knew she shouldn't. 'I was talking more about flowers, *actually*. And how there's a whole language of flowers – each one has a special meaning.'

'Riiiight.' Simon managed to make the single word sound as though he was completely bored. 'I'm sure that's a lot of help when you're working in the garden.' Seeing her open her mouth to respond, he added, 'But you can't help it, you're a girl. Girls like pretty flowers and stuff like that. It's not proper gardening.'

'*Proper gardening*?' Kate couldn't believe it. 'What are you talking about? I do proper gardening. You couldn't live with my grandpa and *not* do it!'

'Proper gardening,' said Simon, straightening up, 'is heavy work. Lifting, weeding, digging – back-breaking stuff.' His gaze swept over her deliberately. 'You don't look like you're strong enough. You'd better stick to arranging flowers.'

Kate felt like she was ready to explode. 'You say that like it's easy! Let me tell you, flower arranging takes years of training and loads of talent to do it well. I should know – my mum's a florist.' *I said 'is'*, she thought wildly, *why didn't I say 'was'?* 'Besides, you don't know anything about me. I'm stronger than I look.' She glared at him.

Simon shrugged. His voice dropped though it still kept its sarcastic edge. 'You probably potter around a bit, don't you? Pick beans and things? I'm re-designing our garden at home. I'm going to be a landscape gardener when I leave school.'

'So?' Kate wished lunch break was over so that she would have an excuse to leave. She cast around for something biting to say. 'I bet your parents are just *thrilled* that they've got cheap labour to do their work for them.' She was delighted to see Simon flush pink.

'They are, thank you,' he said.

'And they'll be so *proud* when you exhibit at Chelsea,' Kate went on, unable to resist.

Simon's eyes flashed. 'They will. That's what I've told my father. He wants me to be a research chemist, like him. But I'll show him.'

Kate was momentarily diverted. 'A research chemist? What does he research?'

'Why?' His gaze was hostile. 'Diseases. Cancer, that sort of stuff.'

Cancer. Kate felt as though all the breath had left her body. The one word that could still reduce her to a frozen mess of awfulness. 'Oh.'

'He's working on a new wonder drug. Wants me to follow in his footsteps.' Simon gave an unamused laugh. 'I can't think of anything more boring.'

'*Boring?*' Kate couldn't help repeating it aloud. 'A cure for – cancer – is *boring?*'

Simon's dark eyes met hers, fierce and uncompromising. 'It is if you don't want to do it.'

Kate had to look away. She couldn't believe what she was hearing. If Simon's father really thought he was good enough to be a research chemist, like him, then Simon must be very clever indeed. How could he possibly throw away the chance to discover something so amazing? For *landscape gardening*? 'I'm –

um – going to the loo,' she mumbled, getting up. *I can't be near him*. She was terribly afraid she might cry.

Locking the door to the cubicle, she stared at the floor. *Why did I say Mum is a florist? Why did I pretend she's still alive?* She pressed her hands against her closed eyes and tried to calm down. *Get a grip. He's just saying stuff to annoy you. You just have to rise above it*. That's what Anpa would say. She concentrated on her breathing. In – two – three – four. Out – two – three – four.

By the time she came out, Kate was feeling more in control. In fact, she was almost surprised at herself. She'd become so good at withdrawing from confrontation these past three years, from any situation that might get heated. She'd built some very strong barriers between herself and the rest of the world – and one morning with Simon had punched a hole through them all!

Apprehensive, she was relieved to find Simon absorbed in a book on gardening when she got back to the yard. He didn't look up. The passageway was sheltered and the sun was directly overhead. Kate wondered how on earth she would fill the next half an hour. She sighed and sat down on her toadstool, leaning her back against the fence and looking upwards. Maybe sitting down for a bit was a good idea. After all, her back *was* aching from standing at that potting bench. She closed her eyes. What would Anpa be doing right now? Snoozing in the garden, she was willing to bet. Though if anyone caught him at it, he'd always deny it. 'Just resting my eyes,' he'd protest. Kate smiled. The snoring gave him away every time!

'Kate. *Kate.*'

'Huh?' Kate struggled to open her eyes, realizing that her back had stiffened up even further. 'What?'

'You were asleep,' Simon told her. A small smile hovered around the corners of his mouth, quickly suppressed.

Kate straightened up immediately. Was he *smirking*? 'Asleep! What are you talking about?'

'It's time to get back to work.'

'Don't be ridiculous, it's only . . .' Kate glanced at her watch. 'Oh my . . . How did that happen?'

Simon stood up. 'We have to go.'

Kate followed him back to the staff room, hastily rubbing her face and wondering with some shame exactly how long she had been asleep. And – oh dear – had she been snoring? Drooling? *In front of Simon?* How completely embarrassing!

If Janet noticed that Kate was quieter than usual as she gave them instructions, she didn't comment.

Simon was sent to help Jason move some bird tables and garden ornaments from the delivery area to the display shelves. Kate was told to finish her job from this morning pricing herbs before going back to continue potting up the aquilegia. She was very relieved that she wouldn't be working with Simon again that day.

Tomorrow, she thought. *Tomorrow I'll deal with him better. Tomorrow I won't let him annoy me; I'll just rise above it. After all, I know what he's like now. He thinks he's better than everyone else. I just have to pretend I haven't heard anything he says.*

But at the back of her mind was the painful, twisting memory of Simon saying that finding a cure for cancer was *boring* . . . when it was the one thing that could have saved her mother.

Chapter 4

Periwinkle

Megan stretched out in her reclining chair and sighed with pleasure. 'That's better. Peace and quiet in the summer sun. No pest of a brother bombing around. No school, no homework. A perfect Sunday. I could so doze off right now.' She sniffed. 'Something smells gorgeous.'

'It's the rose bush.'

'Did I tell you Jake gave me roses for my last birthday?' Megan smiled, her eyes closed. 'It was just after we got together. He's so romantic.'

Kate didn't know what to say. 'Wow.'

'I know. Red roses.'

Red roses mean *I Love You*, thought Kate in her head. Somewhere deep inside, she felt a small pang of jealousy. *It must be so nice to have someone feel that way about you.* Would anyone ever feel that way about her? She couldn't imagine it somehow.

Anpa, digging in a nearby bed, sat back on his heels. 'That's looking better.'

Kate leaned forward. 'You missed a dandelion. Just there.'

Anpa pulled a face. 'I meant to. It's for the wild rabbits.' Then he bent to dig it up, muttering.

Megan laughed. 'You two are so funny. I wish my grandpa was as cool as yours.'

Anpa shook his head. '*Cool*. Honestly, you young people.'

Kate rolled her eyes. 'Take no notice of him, Megan. He's just a *fuddy-duddy*. He said so himself.'

Megan laughed again. 'It's all right. I'm used to you now, aren't I, Mr Lumsden?'

Anpa looked at her fondly. 'You know I'm only pulling your leg.'

'Why don't you come and sit with us for a bit, Anpa?' Kate suggested. 'I'll get you a chair.'

'No, no. Lots to do today. I'll have a sit down later.'

Kate slid off her chair. 'Then let me help.'

'Certainly not!' He looked almost fierce. 'You work hard enough during the week as it is. You have a sit down and talk to your friend. Make the most of it.' He turned to Megan. 'When are you all off then?'

'Tomorrow morning,' replied Megan. She stretched

49

out her slim legs and wriggled her pink polish-tipped toes. 'I can't stay long today, Mum's going frantic about the packing because Owen keeps taking stuff out of the suitcases and hiding it.'

Kate grinned. Owen was Megan's five-year-old brother and a human tornado. 'I'm surprised your mum didn't make you bring him along.'

'She sent him off to a friend's for the afternoon. She asked them especially to take him swimming and wear him out as much as possible.' Megan laughed. 'Everyone's hoping he'll sleep on the plane tomorrow and not cause mayhem.'

'As if!'

'And I just *know* she's going to put him between me and Jake. He loves Jake, thinks he's the best thing in the world. So Mum's hoping Jake will be able to keep Owen occupied all the time, so that *she* won't have to do it.' Megan sighed. 'Bang goes any proper conversation, or anything.'

Kate said nothing. Megan and Jake were such a perfect couple. They had danced together since they were little, but it was only since Christmas that they'd started going out. When she was with Jake, Megan changed in subtle ways – her smile became brighter, her laugh more carefree. Kate was fascinated by the way Megan seemed to glow when Jake was around.

It felt like a kind of magic. *If I found a boyfriend one day, would that happen to me too?* She shook herself. 'You'll have lots of time with Jake in Cyprus though, won't you? I mean, three weeks . . .'

'Yeah, I really hope so. We've been so busy recently with training, it feels like we haven't spent much time chilling out together.' Megan grinned again and pushed her sunglasses into her glossy red hair. 'I'm aiming to come back with a wicked tan.'

Anpa made a noise that he hurriedly turned into a cough.

'What did I say this time?' demanded Megan, amused. 'Oh, I know – wicked! Mr Lumsden, you're going to have to learn some new words.'

'I know those words just fine, Megan Hirst,' said Anpa, getting to his feet with difficulty. 'And I don't see what's wrong with the things they used to mean. You might as well take a word like – like "turnip" – and make it mean "wonderful". Humph.'

Megan gave a shout of laughter. 'Turnip! Brilliant! I'm going to use that this holiday and see if anyone notices. Can you imagine? "The pool here is turnip!"' She burst into giggles. Kate's grandfather smiled indulgently and headed off to the garden shed, muttering something about needing a spade.

A memory burst in upon Kate: a glittering blue

pool, its edges stretching off into infinity, as though the water and sky merged together. Her father, shouting with delight as he ran towards it, sending up water droplets over three metres high as he splashed in. Then turning to call to her mother, who approached more daintily, her floral bikini contrasting with the healthy glow of her skin. Her mother, reaching down to take Kate's hand to help her into the water, smiling all the time, the shimmering light dancing across her face. *Come on in*, she said. *Hold my hand.*

Where was it? Kate knew she was young at the time – was it Turkey? France? It didn't matter. Holidays like that would never happen again. She squashed the memory with a tightening of her lips.

Megan saw her friend's downcast expression and misunderstood. 'Hey, don't look like that. I'll be back before you know it. Besides, you'll be so busy working, the time will fly by. And when I come back, we'll go out and do stuff.'

'Yeah.'

Megan reached out. 'And you keep in touch, OK? Text me. I can still get texts out there, you know. Let me know how everything's going.' She squeezed Kate's hand. 'Especially if there's any gossip! Or any boys. You know it's my mission to find someone as perfect for you as Jake is for me.'

Kate made an effort to smile. 'You know no one could be as perfect together as you two. Besides, I'm going to be at Tilworths all summer, so no chance of meeting any nice boys.'

'I thought you said you were working with a boy? What's his name?'

'Simon.'

'That's the one. What's he like?'

Kate pulled a face. 'Horrible. Rude. Thinks he's better than everyone else.'

'Oh no.' Megan looked sympathetic. 'I'm really sorry. Bad luck. I knew someone like that once.' She grimaced. 'Although I reckon he wasn't really like it underneath. It was all for show. Maybe Simon isn't as bad as you think?'

Kate raised her eyebrows. 'Unlikely. Anyway, I haven't had to see him much over the last couple of days, so hopefully we'll keep doing different jobs.'

'I can't believe you've got an actual, proper job,' remarked Megan. 'It sounds so grown-up.' She glanced at her watch. 'I must go. For some weird reason, Mum wants to clean the house at the same time as packing. She says it's nice to come home to a clean house! Mad. I've got to do the hoovering, so I'd better get a move on. Don't be freaked out if you see a light on in our

house while we're away. Mum's persuaded the neigh-
bours to come round sometimes to make it look like
there's someone there.' She grinned. 'Another reason
why she wants the house spotless, I guess. Though
Mrs Burstow is so short-sighted she wouldn't be able
to see the dirt anyway!'

Kate gave her a hug. 'Have an amazing time. And
say hi to Jake for me.'

'Will do. And listen – don't work too hard, OK?
And don't let that Simon boy get to you. Maybe he'll
loosen up a bit, you never know.'

Kate nodded, suddenly feeling quite sad that
Megan was going to be away for so long.

Megan called out a cheerful goodbye to Anpa
as she passed the shed. The side gate clicked shut
behind her, and Anpa stuck his head out of the doorway. 'Lemonade?' he suggested.

♥

'I was thinking,' said Anpa as they sipped their
lemonade in the shade of the apple tree, 'about a new
cold frame to protect the bulbs. We might be able to
get one cheap at this time of year.'

'I could use my discount at Tilworths,' suggested
Kate.

'Discount?' Anpa sat up straight. 'What kind of discount?'

'Twenty per cent off.'

'Well! How about that!' He immediately started muttering under his breath. 'Garden twine, and of course a new fork because the handle keeps falling off . . . and the trellis is rotting at the bottom—'

'Stop, stop!' said Kate, laughing. 'We haven't got room for loads of new stuff!'

Her grandfather gazed out across their garden. 'There's a lot of things could do with replacing or repairing though.'

Kate followed his gaze. Their garden wasn't really all that big, but every available inch was used. Up by the house were three large beds. When her mother had been alive, all three had been stuffed to bursting with flowers for cutting, but now only the first bed was for flowers. Anpa had commandeered the other two for vegetables and fruit: potatoes, squash, beans, peas, rhubarb, raspberries . . . They provided food for dinner all year round. Right at the bottom of the garden there was a small patch of lawn (the only bit Anpa would allow) dotted with four fruit trees and a garden shed for all the tools.

A couple of years back, Kate's father had bought a second-hand storage freezer which he installed in the garage. If they had too many strawberries or beans or carrots, they simply put them into bags and froze them. Megan had been astonished when, visiting Kate's house for the first time in January, Kate had offered her a strawberry smoothie made with home-grown strawberries!

Anpa was very impressed with the freezer when Nick had brought it home. 'Big enough to store all sorts of things,' he commented, his eyes gleaming.

Kate looked at him curiously. 'What do you mean?'

'Oh, fruit and veg, of course,' he said, not meeting her gaze.

'Anpa . . .'

'All right, all right. You could get a couple of pigeons, maybe a rabbit or two, a pheasant . . .'

Kate's jaw dropped in horror. 'What are you talking about? Where from?'

He glared back at her. 'Don't look at me like that. When I was young, that's what people did around my village. Into the woods on a Saturday, take a couple of pot shots, see what you could pick up.'

'You went into the woods and *shot* wild animals?'

'Not *me*,' said Anpa, sounding disappointed. 'I wasn't allowed. When I was old enough to learn, they'd stopped all that. People were getting caught.'

Kate dragged her thoughts back to the present. The sun was shining and she was sitting in the garden with her favourite grandfather. She ignored the tiny nagging hurt that was always there, always inside of her; the hurt that reminded her of her mum. Instead, she looked over towards the large flower bed, the nodding heads of blue, pink, white, peach. The colourful blooms gave her a sense of calm and beauty. No wonder her mother had loved working with them so much.

'Hello?' Her dad's voice was carried down the garden on a breeze. 'Anyone home?'

Anpa beamed. 'Didn't think you'd be back yet.'

'Air conditioning broke down,' explained Nick as he came to join them. 'It got too hot to work in the office.'

Anpa's face fell, and Kate knew how he felt. She'd been hoping her father had come home early just to spend time with his family, but he hadn't done it by choice.

'Ooh, lemonade.' Nick saw the glasses in their hands. 'Good idea. I'll go and get some.'

'You could get ice cream while you're in the kitchen,' pointed out Anpa. 'Since you're up.'

Nick nodded. 'Back in a minute.' He returned with three choc-ices and a glass of lemonade.

'Thanks, Dad.' Kate smiled at him. She shouldn't be angry with him really; he worked very hard and she should just be grateful he was home at all.

'Got some good news,' Nick told them as he sat on the grass and unwrapped his choc-ice. 'The MD is so impressed with my recent work he's giving me an extra bonus this Christmas. Should be quite substantial, he said.'

'That's great, Dad.' Kate felt pleased. 'Would it be enough for a holiday, do you think? It's just that Megan . . .' She trailed off.

'That's a good idea,' Anpa butted in. 'With the overtime you've been putting in and the bonus you could go somewhere really nice.'

'You'd have to come too, Anpa.'

Her father was unsure. 'I don't know, love. Things are very busy at the moment, and there's a possible merger coming up early next year. Let's see how it goes, shall we?'

Anpa pressed the point. 'Kate hasn't had a proper holiday for ages.'

Nick scowled. 'I'm doing my best. There just hasn't been time. I can't just drop everything, you know.'

'But if you gave them enough notice . . .' Kate suggested. 'I mean, if we booked it now . . .' Her heart thumped. 'Maybe we could get some brochures from

the travel agent and pick somewhere really nice . . .'
Like we used to.

Her father gave her a rueful smile. 'Let's see, shall
we? No point rushing into anything. Besides, we
might want to use the money for something else. A
new car maybe.'

Kate stared. 'A new *car*? What's wrong with the one
we've got?'

'Nothing, nothing.' Nick shrugged, looking a little
uncomfortable. 'Only it'd be nice to have something a
bit newer, don't you think? More up-to-date?'

A hard knot formed in Kate's throat and for a
moment she thought she might cry, but then she realized it was anger she felt. 'You don't need a new car,'
she told her father crossly. 'It works fine. But I want
to go on holiday, like everyone else. I want to go away
somewhere hot, like Megan and Jake. Why can't we
do that?'

Her father looked a little surprised. It wasn't like
Kate to argue like this. 'They rely on me at work . . .'

'*Mum* would have taken time off.'

There was a shocked silence and even the birds
seemed to hold their breath. Kate glared at her father,
hardly able to believe she'd actually voiced her inner
thoughts. But he gazed stonily at the ground, refusing to look up at her or even reply. Anpa sat very still.

When it became clear that Nick wasn't going to say anything in response, Kate got to her feet. Fine – if her own father couldn't talk about going on something as simple as a *holiday*, then . . . then she didn't want to talk to him anyway.

Kate stomped back to the house, feeling the hard knot in her throat threaten to dissolve into tears. *Nobody cares what I want*, the voice thundered in her head. *And maybe I won't stay quiet and meek any more.*

♥

Kate hoped very much that Anpa wouldn't come to see if she was all right. She didn't want to see anyone right now. She felt horrible, as if something was tearing at her insides and chewing on her heart. Everything in her room suddenly looked wrong: the pictures on the walls, the bedside lamp, the iPod dock – even the duvet cover. Everything seemed to be silently shouting at her, making her head hurt. She huddled down in the middle of the floor, her legs tightly crossed and her arms over her head. If she could shut the outside world out . . . maybe somewhere still inside her head she would find her mother.

I can't remember what she looked like any more,

Kate thought miserably to herself. *I see her in photos but I can't conjure up a memory of her face. How can that be? She's only been gone three years, how can I be forgetting her already? Does it mean that eventually, as the years go by, she'll be wiped from my mind altogether?* The thought hurt more than anything and Kate cried quiet, terrified tears into her sleeves, hugging herself and trying to imagine that her own arms were those of her mother's.

When finally the awful overwhelming pain sub-sided, Kate wiped her eyes and stared unseeingly at the wall. The worst thing was feeling so lonely all the time. Megan was a good friend, but she couldn't know how it felt. Nobody could. Kate remembered how her old friends had been sympathetic at first. Tasha had been so upset for her, she had cried herself. She'd brought Kate sweets and magazines to cheer her up; had tried to get her to 'come out with us all' to 'take your mind off it'. But Kate had refused and, after a while, a coldness had crept into their friend-ship. Tasha wanted to talk about celebrities, a new hairstyle, shopping in London. Her other friends laughed and joked with her about shared experi-ences, but Kate couldn't bring herself to pretend she cared. Didn't they know how when someone you loved died, everything around you faded into insignificance? Why would she care about Cheryl Cole or Justin Bieber? How could she care about shoes when she didn't have a mother any more?

And one day she'd actually said as much to Tasha. Tasha's response was swift and unexpected. 'Get *over* yourself, Kate. I have tried to be sympathetic, but honestly! It's been months and months and you're still crying the whole time. You've changed, you're no fun any more. If you want to be miserable for the rest of your life, go ahead, but don't make me miserable too.'

Kate had been shocked to the bottom of her heart. How could a best friend say things like that? Hurt and humiliated, she had spat some retort and that had been the end of their friendship.

Kate hadn't really helped out in the garden when her mother was alive, but when Anpa moved in, she found herself outside more and more often. Weeding, pruning, digging, planting . . . these were all activities that made no demands on her emotions. The beans didn't care how she felt; the lawn didn't talk to her about shopping. The flowers bloomed every year with reassuring regularity, and Anpa was good company. Sometimes he talked; sometimes he didn't. They could spend a whole afternoon with each other and barely exchange more than fifty words. Over time, the raw, jagged grief dulled to an ache, and it was easier to remember to breathe; to form sentences; to do her homework.

And then, less than a year ago, she had met Megan, who had moved to the area and was looking for a friend. They didn't have much in common really, but somehow Kate had been reassured by Megan's self-confidence. It reminded her of the old Kate, the one who made up games, took the lead. Megan had a spark of adventure in her too – a spark that she mostly channelled into her dancing, which amazed Kate the first time she'd seen it. Megan seemed to exude all the passion that Kate had once felt for life but had lost since her mother died. Kate had watched enviously, knowing that the barriers she had raised made that kind of freedom impossible now.

Kate blinked. The light was moving up the wall, which meant the sun was low in the sky and it must be nearly dinner time. With a twinge of guilt for what she had said to her father earlier, she got up stiffly from the floor. She supposed she should apologize – *But why should I?* she thought rebelliously. *What I said was true. Mum took time off for holidays, and she was very busy at work. She made sure she had time for us as a family.*

No, Kate decided, she wouldn't apologize. She'd

had enough of being quiet and accepting of what everyone else wanted. She would wait to see if her father said anything, 'But I bet,' she said out loud to her reflection, 'that he doesn't. He'll pretend it never happened, and everything will go on just as before.'

Things weren't about to change just because of something she'd said.

Chapter 5

Gloxinia

When Kate arrived for work on Wednesday, there was a large board over one of the windows of the shop. 'What happened?' she asked Carol, who was on the till by the entrance.

Carol frowned. 'Someone threw a brick at it yesterday evening. Smashed it completely. Mike's ordered a new pane of glass but it won't come for another week.'

'That's horrible,' said Kate, staring at the brown board.

'It certainly is,' agreed Carol. 'I can't believe it's still going on.'

'Still going on? Oh . . .' Kate remembered. 'There was a rock on the roof, wasn't there?'

'That's only the half of it.' Carol leaned forward. 'Things have been going missing from the shop – little bits here and there – but someone's definitely stealing. I can't be everywhere at once, and to put cameras up would be really expensive. What with that and the vandalism – did you know someone spray-painted a swear word on the fence two months ago?'

'No.' Kate was shocked.

'Well, Mike sorted it out pretty quickly. But this one's worse than usual. You can tell it's getting the two of them down. It's not nice to think that someone's got it in for you.'

'You mean . . .'

'I think it's personal,' Carol said, nodding. 'I mean, why would anyone keep coming back and making mischief?'

'But who . . . ?'

'I don't know. But the police are being absolutely useless.' Carol looked cross again. 'They just come and give us a crime number and then go away again. It's all very well, but all these bits and pieces add up. Mike and Janet have to cover the cost somehow.' She glanced around. A customer was heading over to the till. 'Don't say anything,' she told Kate. 'I mean, there's nothing we can do.'

Kate nodded and made her way through the shop to the staff room to drop off her bag. *What a horrible thing to put up with*, she thought. *Poor Mike and Janet.*

I wonder who on earth would want to do something like that to them?

♥

There was hardly a cloud in the sky and by mid-morning, the sun was scorching the garden centre. Kate wiped her forehead. She and Simon were watering the plants on display. It was a long job because there were so many rows and each one was piled with plants. Janet had been quite strict when she gave them their instructions. 'Each plant is worth something,' she told them. 'If you miss out one pot when watering, that plant won't make it and we'll lose money. So don't do a half-hearted job. Watering is boring but it's also probably the most important thing you'll do here.'

Kate had shot a look at Simon, who was star-ing at the ground and nodding. The two of them hadn't had much of a chance to talk in the last week because they had been given different jobs to do and sometimes even their lunch times hadn't coincided. Kate hadn't minded – after their disastrous first day together, she didn't feel at all inclined to get to know him any better! She missed Megan, who always knew how to make her feel more positive about awkward situations. But Megan was now sunning herself beside a pool in Cyprus.

'Shall I do the top end with the alpines and herbaceous?' Kate had suggested. 'And you start down the bottom with the fruit trees and conifers? Each do half?'

Simon had nodded. 'No problem.'

Kate felt grateful that she had been given a watering job. The cold water rushing through the hose helped to cool her down and she splashed herself once or twice on purpose. She noticed vaguely that Simon had gone back to the water tap and was fiddling with the hose connector. He looked annoyed. Something must have gone wrong with it, but Kate didn't particularly want to go and offer help. She tried to pretend she wasn't sneaking glances at him and so didn't even notice the girl who had come up behind her. 'Excuse me. Um . . .'

'Oh, sorry!' Kate turned. The girl was about her own age with brown hair cut into a short bob and lively blue eyes. 'Can I help you?'

'My mum sent me,' the girl said. She rolled her eyes dramatically. 'She's landscaping the garden, or so she *says*, but so far all she's done is dig stuff up and make a big mess. She told me to get some things for her, but the trouble is I have no idea what any of it is or where to find it.' She pulled a face. 'Can you give me a hand?'

Kate smiled, amused. 'Of course. Let me just switch this off.' She hurried over to the water tap, where Simon was still kneeling on the ground.

He looked up, frowning. 'You finished already?'

'No, got to help a customer.' She hesitated. 'Is everything OK?'

'Plastic washer in the connector has snapped,' he said gloomily. 'The water keeps spurting out everywhere. I'm trying to mend it.'

'Maybe Jason could help?'

Simon shook his head. 'I'll sort it.'

'You can use my hose in the meantime.'

'No, I've said I'll sort it.'

Irritated by his snappy tone, Kate walked back to the waiting girl. Then she realized she probably still looked cross, so she made an effort to smile. Janet wouldn't be pleased if the customers said she had unfriendly staff. 'Right, what do you need then?'

But the girl was gazing over Kate's shoulder. 'That boy,' she said. 'Is he – does he work here too?'

Kate was puzzled. 'Yes – why, do you know him?'

The girl shook her head. 'No, no. It's just that – well. *Wow*. You know?'

'Uh . . .'

'Oh, come *on*.' The girl leaned towards her with a

conspiratorial expression. 'He's gorgeous!'

'Is he?'

'What's his name?'

'Simon,' replied Kate, wondering if she should even be telling this strange girl something like that.

'Simon,' said the girl wistfully. '*Simon*.' She seemed lost in thought.

Kate glanced back at Simon, but the sight of him didn't make her heart flutter one bit. She just felt mildly cross again. 'Should we be getting on with your list?' she prompted after a moment.

The girl blinked. 'Oh gosh, sorry. Yes, of course. I'm Libby, by the way.'

'Kate.'

'You must think I'm mad,' said Libby. 'I can't help it. I just love boys, don't you?'

'Er . . .'

'My friend Tania says I'm boy-crazy,' Libby confided. 'I'm sort of between boyfriends at the moment.'

Between boyfriends? thought Kate. *What does that even mean?*

'So I'm on the lookout,' Libby went on. 'And that Simon – wow. What gorgeous skin. Like he's from the Mediterranean or something. Is he Spanish?'

'I don't know,' said Kate, beginning to feel vaguely

irritated by Libby's persistence. 'I don't think so.'

'Has he got an accent?' asked Libby hopefully. 'I love accents.'

'No. Listen, do you want to show me your list? Only I've got the watering to do . . .'

'Of course.' Libby pulled a face. 'Sorry, I know I get a bit carried away sometimes. Here you go. I can't read half of what she's written, but that could be just because I don't understand what she means.'

'Lawn feed,' read Kate. 'Two pots fennel, one English lavender, one sage.'

'That says sage?' Libby exclaimed. 'I thought it said soap!'

'Thistle seed,' went on Kate. 'Red spring onion seeds. Small bag ericaceous compost.'

'Eri-what?'

'It's a type of soil for certain plants, like heathers.'

Libby stared at her. 'Wow. You know your stuff, don't you?'

Kate felt pleased. She wished Simon had been close enough to hear Libby's comment. 'I do a lot of gardening.'

'No kidding. Well then' – Libby grinned at her – 'you're my new best friend.'

♥

By the time Kate had finished finding all the things on Libby's list, Simon had managed to fix his hose and had watered not only his half of the plants but Kate's half too. 'Oh!' said Kate in surprise. 'I didn't realize I'd taken such a long time.'

Simon straightened up from his position on the ground, where he had been re-labelling clematis plants. 'I thought it would be easier for me to do it all.'

Reluctantly Kate said, 'Well, thanks, that's really nice of you.'

Simon chewed his lip. 'Janet went on about good customer service on my first day. She said it was more important than anything else – people come back if they've been treated well.'

'That's true.' Kate nodded. 'We've always come here, even though Parchester West is a bigger centre. But this has a friendlier feel to it.' Looking at him, she suddenly remembered what Libby had said about Simon. Did he really have gorgeous skin? She hadn't noticed before, but then she didn't usually notice things like that. It was a sort of golden colour . . .

'Why are you staring at me?'

In confusion, Kate started to babble. 'Oh, sorry, was I staring? I was just thinking about . . . well, never mind. So what are you doing now then? Do you know what I'm supposed to do next?'

Simon raised his eyebrows. 'I'm labelling these plants. I don't know what you're supposed to do. You'd better go and ask Janet.'

'Right.' Kate turned and went, unable to look Simon in the eye. How embarrassing to be caught staring at him! She didn't even like him! What would he think of her now? 'That girl!' muttered Kate to herself. 'Now she's got me doing it too!'

She *definitely* wasn't going to tell Simon that Libby fancied him.

♥

'You can't be serious,' Kate heard Janet say as she let herself into the staff area.

'What choice do we have?' Mike's voice came in response. He sounded frustrated. 'He's very determined, Janet.'

'I don't care how determined he is, we're not taking that offer. You said yourself it's an insult!'

'That was before I looked at the accounts again . . . this place is sinking.'

'But it's everything we've worked for!'

Kate hesitated in the narrow passageway. This

didn't sound like a conversation she should walk in on. Janet and Mike obviously hadn't heard her come through the security door, but if she went out again, she couldn't be sure they wouldn't hear the door click shut. What should she do?

Undecided, Kate stood still, unable to help over-hearing.

Janet's voice had dropped. She sounded as though she were pleading. 'Mike, when we bought this place, it was nothing, you know it was. We've spent our whole lives building it up. We can't let it go.'

'It's not as simple as that,' Mike said. 'This place is bleeding money at the moment. We might be better off cutting our losses.'

'But what he's offering this time wouldn't cover the cost of the land, let alone the business! At least his last offer was reasonable – this one is just ridiculous!'

'We can't go backwards. We turned down the last offer.'

'And we're going to turn down this one too.'

'Things have changed,' said Mike reluctantly. 'We're worse off than we were a few months ago. I know it's unfair, but this might be the best offer we'll get.'

'But you know he'll just knock everything down!' cried Janet. 'He doesn't *want* the garden centre. He wants the land, so that he can build even more of his dull houses, all in dull rows, with their dull back gardens and dull driveways.'

Mike sighed. 'I can't say I like the man any more than you do, Janet, but we have to look at things objectively. This is business.'

'People like Dimitri Ballios shouldn't *be* in business,' Janet said vehemently. 'They trample over little folk like us. Who does he think he is, anyway?'

'A property developer with lots of money,' Mike told her. 'And how long have you been talking about wanting to retire before we're too old to enjoy it? This would be that opportunity.'

'But Mike, all our hard work . . . it would have been for nothing!'

'No it wouldn't. But the centre is losing money, Janet, you know that. The recession has hit us badly. We're struggling as it is. And all these petty things, the bricks through the windows, the thefts . . . ' He sighed. 'I know it's getting you down as much as it is me. It's the last straw. Maybe this is our way out.'

'You *want* to give up,' Janet accused him, sounding tearful. 'You've already made up your mind!'

'No I haven't! I just think we should take this offer seriously. We might not get another one – or, if we do, it'll be even lower. We've only got a few days to decide.'

Kate reached for the handle, wondering if she could slip out silently, but the floor creaked under her and she froze.

'I am *not* selling this place to someone like Dimitri Ballios,' Janet said obstinately. 'He is a parasite. He makes promises and then breaks them. I don't care what you say about business, you don't treat people like that.' Her voice wobbled. 'And this place is worth more to me than money.'

Mike sighed again. 'All right, we'll reject the offer. But if we don't come up with a way to make more money soon, we're looking at ruin anyway.'

'I will think of something,' said Janet firmly. 'Somehow.'

Kate had stood and listened to the whole conversation, feeling more and more uncomfortable. But they seemed to have finished, so she hastily pushed open the security door behind her and pulled it shut again with an audible click.

Mike, coming out of the little staff room, caught sight of her in the passageway. 'Oh, Kate. Everything OK?'

'I've come to ask Janet what I should do next,' Kate said, hoping very much that he believed she'd only just arrived.

'Right, right,' Mike said, glancing back at the staff

room. 'Er – probably not a good moment to ask her, to be honest. She's – having a rest for a minute. Go and talk to Carol instead. I think she was muttering about needing some help today.' He opened the door for her and then remembered something. 'Oh, but before you do, Kate, could you give this to Simon?' He pulled out something small and black from his pocket. 'It's that spare washer for the hose he was wanting. Tell him we did have the right size after all.'

'All right.' Kate hesitated. 'Is Janet OK?'

'She's fine, fine,' Mike said, trying to sound cheerful. 'Just overworked. Aren't we all?'

Kate smiled back but once she was out of sight of Mike, the smile vanished. She knew she shouldn't have listened to the conversation. It was none of her business whether the Tilworths sold their garden centre or not. But Kate felt a terrible sadness at the thought that one of her favourite places might close – worse, be knocked down entirely and replaced with houses! And it sounded as though it wasn't a good deal at all – Janet seemed to think they'd lose everything they'd worked for. *It's not fair*, Kate thought angrily. *If you work really hard for something, no one should be allowed to steal it from you.*

She was still worrying about it when she reached

Simon, kneeling by the clematis plants. 'This is for you.'

Simon looked up. 'Oh, thanks. I thought Mike said he didn't have one that size?'

'He said he found it after all.' Kate hesitated. She wanted to talk to someone about what she had just heard, but it wasn't really her place, was it? After all, it had been a private conversation. She had no business telling anyone, and Simon was surely the least sympathetic person to talk to. *But it can't harm to ask him a question, can it?* she thought. 'Simon – what would you do if you wanted to make this place more profitable?'

He looked confused. 'What?'

Kate dug her foot into the gravel path. 'I mean, just for instance. If you wanted to make more money here, what would you do?'

'Why are you asking me?'

'I just wondered . . . It doesn't matter. Forget it.' She turned away.

'No, wait a minute.' Simon had sat back on his heels and was frowning. 'It's just a weird question, that's all. I don't know. Is Tilworths in trouble or something?'

Kate felt alarmed. 'Oh no, I don't think so,' she lied hastily. 'I was just thinking there must be . . .

well, it can't be making that much money . . . the recession . . .' She trailed off lamely, wishing she'd never started the conversation.

But Simon was looking interested now. 'More profit on a place like this? Well, I guess you have to start by asking what customers want. And then thinking about what they might want but don't know they want, if you see what I mean. What you could offer them that other places can't. A new angle, something original.'

Kate stared at him. 'Wow. That sounds . . . clever.'

He shrugged. 'We have a Young Enterprise scheme at school. They did a talk on marketing. It was a bit like that.'

'What people might want but don't know they want,' repeated Kate thoughtfully. 'I suppose . . .'

Simon waited for a moment longer. 'Yeah, well . . . I should probably get back to these . . .'

'Oh! Sorry.' She felt a little embarrassed, as though she'd just been told off for standing around when she should be working. 'Right. I'll – um, see what Carol needs me to do.'

'OK.'

'See you later.'

He nodded, his attention back on the plants.

Kate headed back to the shop, her head buzzing.

The Tilworths *were* in trouble. Janet said she would come up with a new plan to make money. But what was to stop Kate trying to come up with a plan too? And after what Simon had said, she had plenty to think about. Not least the fact that Simon hadn't been rude and annoying at all . . .

Chapter 6

Lilac

'Aren't you going out again?' asked Kate in surprise.

Her father shook his head, smiling. 'I'm taking the evening off. Thought we could do a takeaway and DVD. What do you think?'

Kate was pleased. Maybe he had forgiven her for getting angry about a holiday. It was nice to see him looking a little more relaxed – and a whole evening with Dad! She couldn't remember the last time that had happened. Months, at least.

Anpa snorted. 'As long as it's not that ridiculous *Die Hard* again.' It was one of Nick's favourite films but the last time they had watched it, Anpa had made disbelieving noises and sarcastic comments all the way through. 'Funny how when he shoots at them he always finds his mark, but even when there are three of them firing at him, he dodges them all.'

'That's because he's the hero,' Kate told him.

'It's unrealistic, that's what it is,' Anpa snapped.

Die Hard wasn't exactly Kate's favourite film either but she didn't mind it too much. It was worth it to be able to spend some time with her dad.

'We don't have to watch that,' Nick said. 'I picked up something new today.' He held up the box. 'I thought it might be Kate's kind of thing.'

Kate stared at the DVD box. A girl in an enormous white ball gown gazed excitedly out of the picture. Behind her were two good-looking men, one in a prince's outfit, and a glowering witch. The title *Enchanted* sparkled and glittered. 'It looks like a fairytale.'

'It is,' Nick told her. 'You know, young girl finds the prince of her dreams, all that stuff.'

Kate attempted to smile, but she wondered why on earth her father thought it would be 'her kind of thing'. She had grown out of *Cinderella* and *Sleeping Beauty* a long time ago, after all. Everyone knew real life wasn't a fairytale. Good people died, for one thing. And they didn't come back. Why on earth would her father think she'd be interested in a fairytale? Did he still think she was a little girl?

'At least it doesn't look like it'll have any guns in it,' Anpa said more cheerfully. 'I like a good happy ending.'

'Indian or Chinese?' asked Nick. 'Or pizza?'

'Chinese,' said Kate immediately. 'I'd love some prawn crackers.' She saw her father's face fall slightly. 'Or Indian,' she said quickly. 'I know you like curry. I don't mind really.'

'No, if you'd like Chinese, then that's what we'll have.' He smiled at her and she knew he was making an effort to be cheerful. *Why is it so much harder to talk to each other than it used to be? And why do I feel it's so hard to please him now?*

'As long as I can have black bean sauce with something . . .' Anpa smacked his lips together.

'Fine.' Nick dug around in a drawer for a menu. 'Shall I just order a variety of stuff? And lots of prawn crackers, of course.' He began muttering to himself and writing down numbers.

'Anpa . . .' began Kate, as the two of them plumped down on the sofa. 'What do you know about property development?'

Anpa gave her an astonished glance and then burst out laughing. 'Where's this come from? You been watching that programme on Channel Four?'

'No, not really. I just wondered. I mean, I know people buy a house and do it up and sell it for lots of money. But how rich *are* they?'

'Some of them are very rich indeed,' said Anpa,

sobering. 'Millionaires several times over, if they do it right and get lucky.'

'So does that mean they can basically do what they want if they're that rich?'

'It's certainly true that money opens doors for you,' replied Anpa, frowning. 'Is this about something in particular?'

Her father put down the phone. 'Should be about twenty minutes,' he reported.

'Kate's asking about property development,' Anpa told him.

'I wanted to do that once,' Nick said. He sat down with a sigh. 'There was this end-of-terrace house, a perfect do-it-upper. I could have made a real go of it, I know it. A similar property had just sold for two hundred and fifty thousand pounds in the next street. Two hundred and fifty! And they were only asking a hundred and twenty for this one. It was before I got my promotion at work, too – I was fed up with everything.' He shrugged. 'Oh well.'

'Why didn't you do it?' asked Kate curiously.

Her father reached past her for the TV guide. 'Oh, you know.' His voice took on a slightly strained note. 'Decided in the end it wasn't a good idea.'

Kate had a funny feeling there was something he wasn't saying. 'What did Mum think?'

Nick twitched. 'It doesn't matter.'

He's avoiding talking about her, thought Kate. *Again. As though she never existed.*

'Why are you asking all this anyway?' Anpa wondered.

Kate buried her frustration and told them about the conversation she had overheard at work. 'I think Mike wanted to take the money. But Janet wouldn't sell.'

'Good for her,' said Anpa. 'Sell Tilworths! They've made it a roaring success compared to how it was before.'

'But they said it wasn't making money now.'

'What is?' asked Nick. 'It's a hard time for businesses. Sounds to me like they might do well to take the offer. Before he lowers it again.'

'They shouldn't give in to that kind of pressure,' Anpa said, frowning. 'He should offer them a fair price.'

'But it would still be better than going bankrupt,' argued Nick.

'Do you think that could really happen?' asked Kate. She felt so sad for Mike and Janet. 'They've had all these little attacks, you see. Like spray-painting and bricks through windows. Mike said it was getting them down, making them feel like it's not worth keeping going. I love it there. I couldn't bear it if they closed.'

'A lot of people would feel the same way,' Anpa said, patting her gently on the knee. 'Maybe you could get some local support for the Tilworths, Kate? Make them feel that other people care about them too.'

'Simon said we needed to come up with something new to make money,' Kate said, remembering. 'Think of something that people would want that they didn't know they wanted.'

Nick nodded. 'He's right. It's how you have to think about marketing and sales these days. Give people something they didn't realize they wanted or needed. We use it all the time at work.'

Anpa looked disapproving. 'That's a bit dishonest. Suggesting people should buy things they don't need.'

'It's just how things are these days. It's a competitive market.' Nick looked at his daughter with some respect. 'This Simon of yours sounds like he's got his head screwed on right.'

'He's not *my* Simon,' Kate said sharply.

Her father grinned. 'All right, keep your hair on.'

'I don't even *like* him.'

'Why not? It sounds like he was quite helpful today,' suggested Anpa.

'Yes, but' – Kate felt the need to explain – 'it's the first time he's even been polite to me. I mean, we just don't get on normally. He's a really grumpy boy and he's too arrogant. I didn't like him right from the start.'

Anpa and Nick exchanged glances. 'If you say so,' said her father mildly.

Kate glared. 'What do you mean?'

'Methinks the lady doth protest too much,' added Anpa, trying not to smile.

'I don't know what you're talking about,' snapped Kate. 'That's not even proper English.'

He held up his hands. 'Don't shoot, don't shoot! You say you don't like him. That's fine.'

'I *don't*.'

'OK then.'

Kate looked at them suspiciously. What were they trying to suggest? That she was lying? Why would she lie about not liking Simon? She *didn't* like him, did she? Maybe other girls would – Libby seemed to think he was attractive, she conceded – but Kate couldn't imagine liking someone who was so totally big-headed.

Though he hadn't actually been big-headed today, had he? All that stuff about marketing – he'd said it in quite a helpful way really. Not as though he were showing off or putting her down.

Kate shook her head in irritation. Thankfully, her father and Anpa had dropped the subject and soon the takeaway arrived, wiping the previous conversation out of their minds.

The three of them settled down to watch *Enchanted*, takeaway boxes open on the coffee table in front of them and a huge paper bag of prawn crackers. As the film began, Nick groaned. 'I didn't realize it was a cartoon,' he said. Kate started to wonder whether she would rather have watched *Die Hard* too. But then the princess fell through the magic portal into the real world, and Nick stopped making derogatory comments and instead munched quietly on his special fried rice, his eyes fixed on the screen. He even laughed at the bits with the chipmunk.

There was a part of Kate that kept telling her these things weren't real. And maybe breaking into song was considered acceptable in a Disney film, but people would just think you were mad if you did it in real life. However, as the film went on, Kate found herself swept away by the story. The heroine, who to start with had seemed soppy and annoying, was actually really sweet and innocent. She just wanted everyone to be happy. And if Kate thought about it, surely that was what people wanted in real life too? It was just that other things got in the way.

Of course, there had to be a little girl whose mother had died. *Great, Dad,* thought Kate. *Even when you pick a fairytale, you choose the one with the motherless girl!* She knew Anpa was shooting an annoyed look at her father too. But even something as tragic as that didn't seem to dent the unstoppable enthusiasm of the central character. And it wasn't Dad's fault, Kate reasoned. He wasn't to know, was he? She wondered how she would feel if or when her own father found a new woman in his life. Somehow she didn't think he would find a princess like the one in *Enchanted*. And as the inevitable happy ending unfolded, Kate found herself conflicted with different emotions. There was a part of her that really, really wanted happy endings to be real. Why not, after all? Why shouldn't things turn out all right in the end? But the bitter part of her still snipped away at that hope, saying tartly, *You're not a princess and you're not living in a fairytale. Bad things happen and there's no point pretending they don't. Don't hope for nice things because you'll just be disappointed. You should have learned that by now.*

'Well,' said Anpa, as the final credits rolled, 'that made a nice change from guns and terrorists.' He grinned at the other two. 'Found myself getting quite sentimental there.'

Nick gave a big yawn. 'What shall we do now? We could play a game.'

Anpa chuckled. 'Bed for me, I'm afraid. And you should make the most of a decent night's sleep, Nick.'

Kate's dad pulled a face. 'Don't start, John. We've had a nice evening, let's not bring work up again.'

'Who's bringing it up? I just said it would be a good opportunity to get some sleep for once.'

'I get sleep.'

'Not enough,' muttered Anpa, and then he hastily added, 'Never mind, never mind.' He rubbed his ear. 'Got a bit of a headache. Must be all that sitting in the sun.'

Kate was surprised. Her grandfather never complained of feeling unwell. 'Shall I get you a para-cetamol?'

He hesitated. 'Go on then. Just one.'

Kate glanced at her father. Anpa normally refused all medicine, so his head must be really painful. Nick raised his eyebrows. 'You sure you're all right, John?'

'It's just a headache,' said Anpa. 'I'll be fine in the morning.'

When Anpa had headed off to his room with his paracetamol, Kate gathered up the empty boxes and glasses. 'Don't wash up,' her father told her. 'Just put everything on the side and I'll do it in the morning.'

'Thanks.'

He smiled at her. 'Have you grown again? I feel like I haven't seen you properly in ages.'

Kate bit her lip. 'I guess we haven't spent a lot of time together,' she said quietly.

'Life!' said Nick, attempting a smile. 'So much to do, so little time. I guess it's like that for everyone.'

Not everyone, Kate's mind said rebelliously. *Megan's dad spends the weekends with his family, and he always makes time to watch Megan in her dance shows.* A sudden thought struck her. *Maybe I'm not interesting enough? Maybe if I did dance shows, Dad would make time for me? Maybe that's why he doesn't come home – he thinks I'm boring.*

Another thought followed hard on the first. *Mum was more interesting than me.*

'You all right?' asked Nick, frowning. 'You look like you've got a pain. Have you got a headache too?'

'Uh – yeah,' Kate lied. 'Yeah, a bit.' *I can't tell him what's really wrong. What if it just makes things worse?*

Her father reached for the packet of paracetamol and popped one out. 'Here. You take one too.'

'Thanks.'

He smiled again at her. 'Try not to worry too much

about the Tilworths, OK? Hopefully it'll work out all right.'

'I just wish there was something I could do. I really like working there. I want to help.'

He shrugged. 'Sounds like they need some new ideas fast.'

'I know.' Kate looked down at the paracetamol pill sitting in her hand. 'Mum would have come up with something,' she said without thinking.

There was a soft intake of breath from her father. She didn't dare look up. Was he angry with her for mentioning her mother? Then he sighed. 'Yes, she would,' he agreed. 'Goodnight, Kate.'

'Goodnight, Dad.'

♥

Kate lay in bed, tasting the minty flavour of her toothpaste, and stared at nothing. Thoughts whirled around her head like mist in the morning. She kept hearing the fear in Janet's voice as she talked about losing the centre. New ideas . . . that's what they needed. Some ways to make money.

Kate pulled a face in the darkness. The trouble was, her mother had been the one with imagination, with ideas. She would have come up with a list of solutions in no time, Kate was sure – and they'd all have been brilliant. Her mum had been bright, like a shining star, quick and sharp in her thoughts. But Kate sometimes felt as though her head was full of mud, making it hard to think.

But the Tilworths needed help. Surely Kate must be able to come up with something? She was half Cynthia's daughter, wasn't she? So there must be imagination in there somewhere . . . if she just thought really hard . . .

She turned over to face her clock. It was 10.48 p.m. It wasn't a work day tomorrow, so she could lie in as late as she liked, but Kate knew she would be up early as usual. She'd never been able to stay in bed all day. Megan sometimes talked enthusiastically of Sundays when she'd stayed in her pyjamas until after midday. Kate couldn't do that; she wanted to be up and about, doing things, helping Anpa in the garden . . .

The garden. Was there something there she could use? Her knowledge of gardens . . . She sighed. She doubted there was anything she knew that Janet or Mike hadn't already thought of. Running a business must be so difficult. There was all the stock to buy in, paperwork to fill in, workers to pay . . .

Kate's thoughts turned to Simon. He had been surprisingly helpful about the money angle. At least he hadn't sneered at her, as she'd been afraid he would. Had she been wrong about him? Was he not as arrogant and annoying as she'd first thought? Maybe she should ask him for more help with ideas. But that would mean telling him what she'd overheard, and it was surely meant to be a secret. Kate shook her head even though there was no one to see. No, she wanted to solve this problem herself. She wanted to be the one to present Janet and Mike with the solution to all their money worries, to be the one that everyone thanked . . .

It was all very well being content to work in the background where nobody noticed you, but wasn't it a bit lonely sometimes? Wouldn't it be nice to be noticed for something you'd achieved? *Like Mum . . . People were always going on about how wonderful she was . . . She loved it when they wrote or rang to thank her for her work.*

It would be nice to feel that way too for once.

She reached under her pillow for the photo she always kept there. Her mother's smiling face looked out at her. It usually comforted Kate, but this time she felt as though she needed to ask it a question. 'Mum,' she whispered, 'I don't know if you can hear me, but I need your help.' Cynthia's face beamed into hers, as if to say, *Go on*, so Kate squeezed her eyes tight and thought really hard about Tilworths: the property developer, the fear in Janet's voice, the hard-working staff there . . .

♥

When Kate woke, she was still clutching the photograph. There was a faint scent of lilies in the air. And suddenly, she knew what to do!

Chapter 7

Amethyst

Janet looked sceptical. 'It sounds a bit – I don't know, New Age.'

'But you said yourself how much you'd liked that bouquet my mum did.'

'That's true . . . but there'd be an initial outlay which we couldn't afford.'

'Hardly anything,' said Kate. 'Mostly labels and ribbons, and a few pretty pots. I've been working it out – look.' She showed them a scribbled set of notes. 'I'm sure we can make it a success.'

Janet's expression softened. 'It's lovely that you've had an idea to help, Kate. Maybe we could do one or two to see how it goes.'

Kate shook her head obstinately. 'No, you'd need lots of them to make impact and to give people choice. One or two won't give a high enough profit margin.'

The Tilworths laughed. 'Profit margin?' asked Mike, smiling. 'Why are you worrying about profit margins?'

Kate hesitated. 'I overheard what you said the other day. About the centre being in trouble. I didn't mean to – I'm sorry, it was an accident. But I've been thinking and thinking about how we could make more money.'

'Oh, Kate, that's not something for you to worry about,' said Janet, her eyes suddenly watery with emotion. 'It's our problem, not yours.'

'But I work here,' said Kate. 'And I like it here. And – and I think it should stay open. So I came up with this.' Her heart was thumping so loudly she felt as though Janet and Mike must be able to hear it too. She wasn't used to speaking up like this. 'I really, really think this can work. Because it's sort of gifts and plants in one. And people always want to buy presents for other people – Carol said she sells a lot of stuff in the gift shop.'

Mike was looking bewildered, but Janet suddenly nodded. 'All right. Goodness knows, we've had to take enough risks in the past. Explain it to me again.'

'Hold on a minute . . .'

'Mike, she's got an idea. And it might just work. Think how popular our hanging baskets are every year – we make a lot of money from them. How brilliant would it be if we could bring in that kind of money each month?'

'They're not hanging baskets though, are they?' Mike was still looking puzzled.

'Tell us again,' Janet said to Kate. 'And say it slowly.'

Kate took another breath. 'My mum based her business on the language of flowers. People liked know-ing that there was a hidden message in their bouquet or their basket or whatever. But there's no reason why we couldn't do the same thing here. People love sending messages – look at emails, texts, all that. And everyone loves codes, like spies and invisible ink. So, my idea is to put a flowering plant into a pretty pot and give it a label that explains what the plant means. Like – lilies mean beauty. And heliotrope means devo-tion. And ivy means friendship. I've got lots of books at home about the language of flowers, so we can pick the ones that are most suited to this time of year. If we do handmade labels, with the name of the plant and an explanation of what it means, it makes them all the more special, and we can tie the labels on with ribbons to dress them up a bit.' Kate stopped, out of breath. It was probably the longest speech she'd ever made, and her heart was thumping louder than ever, but Janet and Mike were looking thoughtful.

'We could have different sections,' said Janet

slowly, 'for the different meanings. Love is bound to be the most popular, don't you think?'

'But say you're looking for a birthday present for an aunt,' said Mike. 'You don't want one that means "romantic love", do you?'

'No,' Kate was anxious to answer, 'but you could get one that means happiness or success or elegance or cheerfulness, or—'

'Stop, stop!' Mike held up his hands, smiling. 'I understand.'

'I like it,' said Janet. 'But do you think people will really pay more for a plant that they could buy and put in a pot themselves?'

'It's not the plant we're selling as such, but the idea,' said Mike. 'Right, Kate?'

She nodded. 'And we're saving them the work. It's like trying to work out what message to put in a birthday card. We've done it for them – the flowers say it all.'

'Now that's a slogan I like,' said Janet. '*Flowers Say It All* – we could print that onto a banner and put it above the display.'

Kate felt as though her smile reached right to her ears. She had done it! They were looking at her with a new respect – *this*, then, was what it was like to have ideas that other people loved.

It was a good feeling.

♥

'I think it's a great idea.'

Kate blinked. 'Pardon?'

Simon straightened up from his position on the ground, where he had been repairing the lower shelf of a display unit. 'I said I think it's a great idea. People love hidden meanings and all that kind of thing. They'll pay loads for something they feel is personal. Even when it's cheap rubbish.'

Kate went red. 'This won't be cheap rubbish.'

'I didn't mean that,' Simon said hastily. 'I know it won't. I think it was really clever of you to come up with it.'

'Oh, thanks.' Kate was astonished. He was calling her clever! In her confusion, she mumbled something about it all being down to something he had said anyway.

'What do you mean?'

She tried to pull herself together. 'You remember when you said it was about giving people something they didn't know they wanted? Well, it got me think-ing about people buying presents. And how they want value for money, but also something pretty that *means* something . . .' She trailed off. 'Janet and Mike seem to like the idea, anyway.'

'Of course they do – it's a perfect way to sell flowers.' He looked straight at her. 'It's really original too – well done.'

Kate dropped her gaze in embarrassment. Praise from Simon felt really nice! On an impulse, she let him into her secret. 'I just felt I had to do something to stop that Dimitri man getting Tilworths.'

Simon's eyes widened. 'Who?'

'It was something I overheard. He's a property developer and he wants to buy Tilworths. That's why Janet and Mike need to make more money. Otherwise they might have to sell up.' She glanced at Simon and jumped in shock. It was as though his face had turned to stone. 'Simon?'

He didn't move.

'Are – are you OK?'

'What?' Eventually, he blinked. 'Yeah. Nothing. Got to get on.' He turned away from her.

Kate was taken aback. What a sudden change! One minute he was praising her for her idea, saying how clever she was – and the next it was as though he didn't want to speak to her any more! Or worse, that she didn't exist! She was left opening and closing her mouth helplessly, like some kind of humiliated fish.

Baffled, she turned and walked quickly away. She felt angry with herself – she had got too caught up in liking this new respect from other people; she had forgotten her original assessment of Simon. He was rude and arrogant, and she shouldn't have let her guard down. And she *definitely* shouldn't have told him about the centre being in trouble and the property developer.

It just shows, Kate told herself sternly, *that first impressions are usually the right ones and just because a boy says nice things to you it doesn't mean he's a nice person.*

But it still hurt.

♥

Janet lost no time in putting Kate to work on her new 'Flowers Say It All' idea. She took Kate to a wholesale craft shop at lunch time and bought different types of card, ribbon and glitter to use on the labels. Kate felt a little anxious about the responsibility. She knew she had a good eye for colour and design, but Art had never been one of her best subjects at school and she hoped the labels would look attractive and professional.

'I'm going to send Simon to help you this afternoon,' Janet said. 'He can find all the plants and put them in pots ready for your labels.'

'Oh.' Kate felt panicked. She wasn't sure she wanted to see Simon again just yet, especially after their strained conversation this morning. 'I can manage on my own, it's OK.'

'Don't worry, you can order him around as much as you like,' Janet said with a laugh. 'You're the one in charge. He's just an extra pair of hands, and I want to make sure we can get at least twenty on display as soon as possible. I have a good feeling about this.' She pulled Kate into a sudden hug. 'Thanks, love. Tell you what I'm going to do – get on the phone to the local paper and put an advert in saying we're starting a new line in specialist flower gifts. It shouldn't cost much and hopefully it'll bring in some new customers too.' She let go and grinned at Kate. 'I must go and order the banner. I'll leave you to it. I'm sure they're going to fly off the shelves!'

Kate stood in the staff room alone for a few minutes. It had been a long time since anyone apart from Anpa and her father had hugged her. Even they didn't do it that often. Kate had thought she didn't really like hugs. They made her feel uncomfortable. Janet's hug was different though – she felt warm and soft, like a mum. Kate instinctively felt she'd like to have another hug . . .

Wiping her eyes, she pulled out a slim book called

The Ultimate Language of Flowers from her bag. It was no good getting emotional when there was work to do. Besides, she couldn't afford to make herself vulnerable when Simon was around.

♥

'That looks good,' said Simon, glancing at a label Kate was writing.

Kate pulled a face. 'I don't know. It's not quite how I imagined it.'

'Let me have a look.'

Kate hesitated and then passed it over. She hoped Simon wasn't going to be rude about it just after he'd said something nice again.

The label said:

New Baby
Michaelmas Daisy – Innocence

On the back were the care instructions for the plant.

'Why have you put *New Baby*?' asked Simon.

'Because the daisy means innocence,' explained Kate, 'and I thought that was best suited to a new baby present. You know, instead of buying clothes or a bouquet.' She looked anxious. 'Do you think it's silly?'

'No,' Simon said slowly, 'I think it's clever, actually. I mean, who's going to buy a plant that means innocence unless it's linked to something? You wouldn't give it to someone for their birthday, or to say thank you. New baby seems like a good match.'

'Oh, good.' Kate felt relieved.

'I'm not quite sure about the writing,' Simon said. 'It's a bit wonky.'

Kate bit her lip. He was right, but she wished he hadn't criticized. 'I was trying to make it look artistic.'

'Hmm.' Simon hesitated. 'Do you want me to do the writing?'

Kate was surprised. 'Are you good at it?'

'Dunno, but I'll have a go.'

'All right.' She passed over some paper and a pen. 'Here you are.'

Simon bent over the paper, and Kate was astonished to see him writing 'New Baby' in a beautiful swooping style. 'Wow – that's really good!' She looked at him with new respect.

Simon's neck turned pink. 'It's just practice,' he said. 'My mum used to run this competition for the best baklava, and she always got me to do the certificates for the winners.'

'Best what?'

'Baklava. It's a kind of pastry with honey.' He nodded to the pile of card and glitter. 'Do you want to pass that over and I'll do some more?'

'Thanks.' Kate gave a laugh. 'Not sure what *I'm* supposed to do now.'

'Can't you do the planting and the ribbons?' suggested Simon.

'OK.' She looked at her list of flowers and got to her feet. 'I'm going to go and get some geraniums and campanula. Won't be a minute.'

'What do they mean then?'

'Here.' She gave him the list. 'It's all on there.'

He raised his eyebrows. 'Comfort and gratitude. That's kind of cool.' He looked up at her. 'I've never heard of this language of flowers before, and I've been gardening since I was really small.'

Kate felt a tiny spark of devilry flash into life inside her. 'Maybe you don't know everything,' she said, repeating the words he'd said to her on his very first day. She could tell he remembered it too because his face reddened, but she stuck her tongue out to show she was joking before heading off to find the plants.

It was a very companionable afternoon. It was

strange, Kate reflected as they worked together, how one boy could have two such different sides to him. There was no sign now of the sulky, rude boy she'd met on her first day and who had reacted so oddly when she'd talked about the centre being in trouble. Instead, Simon was actually quite good company, chatting easily about his childhood in the garden. He had some interesting stories too. He'd been to visit a lavender farm and seen how many plants it took to make one tiny bottle of essential oil. 'And it's not even that expensive,' he added, carefully finishing a label that read: *Get Well Soon*. 'Not compared to something like rose oil or jasmine.'

'I can't stand jasmine,' Kate said, wrinkling her nose. 'It sort of gets stuck in my nose.'

'I know what you mean. Lilies do that too.'

'Lilies were my mum's favourite,' said Kate without thinking.

'Were?' asked Simon, reaching for some green card. 'What does she like now then?'

'Oh! Um . . .' *Of course, he thinks Mum is still alive. Should I tell him?* But something in her shrank from the idea – it was too personal. 'Oh, I dunno.'

'My mum likes cacti,' said Simon with a smirk. 'She says they're the only plants that are impossible to kill.'

'To kill?'

'Yeah, she's hopeless with plants. Forgets to water them, puts them next to radiators, that kind of thing. We call her the Plant Killer in our house.'

Kate smiled. 'Who's we?'

'Me and my two brothers and my little sister – and my dad, of course.'

'There are four of you?' Kate stared. She couldn't imagine having that many brothers and sisters. In fact, she couldn't even imagine having one.

'Yeah. My brothers are older though, they don't live at home any more. I just have to put up with my little sister these days. She's ten and she wants to be a princess.' He rolled his eyes. 'She won't wear anything that isn't pink. It drives me mad, but Mum thinks she's a little angel. She gets away with murder.'

'My friend Megan says the same about her little brother.'

'You got any brothers or sisters?'

'No.'

Simon looked surprised. 'I can't imagine being an only child.'

'I can't imagine *not* being one.'

'No wonder you're so serious.'

Kate was taken aback. 'Serious?'

'Yeah. Oh, not in a bad way – I didn't mean . . .'

Simon held up his hands. 'I just meant you seem quite . . . um . . . you don't laugh much.'

Panic gripped Kate. Anxiety made her go on the offensive. 'Neither do you.' Her tone was sharp.

'Well, I guess not . . .'

'And maybe I'd laugh more if you weren't such a know-it-all,' Kate snapped. The words were out of her mouth before she had a chance to think, and as soon as she'd spoken she wished she could take them back.

Simon's face darkened. 'I see. Fine, then. Sorry I spoke.' He got up. 'You obviously don't need my help with these, then. I'm going on my break.'

Kate kept her face downwards so she wouldn't have to see him stalk out. She felt ashamed – how rude of her! For the past three years she'd tried so hard not to show anger; to avoid confrontation. It just made her upset and exhausted – and here she was, saying awful things to Simon when he had just started being nice to her!

She knew she should go after him to apologize, but the thought of it made her feel sick. Instead, with shaking fingers, she tied the beautifully written labels onto the plants she had already prepared, polishing the ceramic pots until they shone and then placing them on a large trolley ready to be wheeled round for display. The label fell off the last plant she lifted. She tied it back on, tighter than before. It was a variegated ivy, with pretty striped leaves. The label read, in Simon's stylish writing: *A Good Friend*.

Kate bit her lip. One thing was for sure – Simon wouldn't be giving her a plant like that any time soon.

Chapter 8

Vervain

'I think it's a fascinating idea,' Anpa said, stretching back in his armchair. They both stared through the patio windows at the rain pouring down. 'Your mother would be delighted her books were being used for something so worthwhile.'

'I hope it'll work,' said Kate fervently. 'They've been on sale a week and we've sold fifteen. Janet says that's a good sign and that things will pick up after tomorrow because the advert will be in the paper. And the banner is due in on Monday, so that will help draw people to the display.'

Outside, the rain thundered down. 'Good for the garden,' said Anpa.

'It'll flatten all my flowers,' said Kate sadly. 'All the Californian poppies will be squashed flat.'

'Make them stronger. Besides, it hasn't rained for two weeks. They need it.'

'I know.'

Her grandfather reached across and squeezed her hand. 'I'm very proud of you, Kate. You're handling this job with such maturity. You seem so grown up, suddenly.'

Kate looked down. She still hadn't apologized to Simon for her horrible words. Every time they'd had to work together, she'd been awkward and difficult to get on with. If Anpa knew how she'd been behaving, he wouldn't say she was grown up or acting with maturity.

'What are you going to spend your earnings on?' Anpa asked.

'I don't know yet. I've just been putting it in my savings account each week.'

Anpa beamed. 'That's excellent. Everyone needs savings for a rainy day.' He looked out at the garden again and laughed.

♥

Later that evening, Kate received a text from Megan.

Hey u! How's trix? HOT HOT HOT here I am melting! Saw some Roman ruins 2day, kinda cool. How's the job going?

Kate stared at her phone. What could she say? If Megan were here, she could have told her about what she'd said to Simon and how awful she felt about it. But it wasn't the sort of thing you talked about in a text. Eventually, she texted back:

Good – have designed my own range of gifts!!! Am new floral specialist!

The reply came through almost instantly.

Knew it! U'll b running the centre by the time I get back!

It made Kate smile. Before she could reply, another text pinged in:

How's that Simon boy? Is he as bad as u thought?

Kate sighed. She could at least confess to Megan how bad she felt. That might help a bit.

No he's not 2 bad after all. But I have bin horrid 2 him. Feel bad.

This time the reply took half an hour.

U were horrid??? Can't imagine it! But perfect optunity 2 kiss and make up, hmm?!!

♥

'No watering today at least,' Simon commented as they arrived for work the next morning. 'That's one boring job we won't have to do.'

'I quite like watering,' replied Kate, and then bit her lip. First conversation of the day and she'd already disagreed with him! 'I mean – uh – yeah, it can be a bit boring.'

'I expect they'll want me round by the fence panels again today,' Simon said. 'I didn't finish everything yesterday.'

'Before you go,' Kate said impulsively, 'I . . . uh . . . I want to apologize.'

He turned to look at her, his dark brown eyes suddenly wary. 'What for?'

'For what I said the other day. I mean . . .' Kate felt her face start to turn red. 'I should have apologized ages ago. I'm really sorry about – what I called you.'

'A know-it-all,' supplied Simon flatly.

'Yes.' She couldn't look at him, it was too embarrassing. 'I didn't mean it. I was – sort of upset – because you were talking about family and stuff, and

. . . and then you said I didn't laugh much . . . and I
should have told you.'

'Told me what?'

She took a breath. 'That my mum . . . passed away.
Three years ago. And I guess I used to laugh more
before . . . before she died. But . . . um . . . it's a bit
difficult now.'

Simon's expression was puzzled. 'I thought you said
she was a florist? And she liked lilies?'

'She did. When she was alive.'

'Oh.'

'So I'm sorry I was horrible to you. I didn't mean to
be. I was just – upset.'

He was nodding now, his face sombre. 'I get it.
I'm sorry too. That's – awful. I'd never have said that
about you being serious if I'd known.'

'I know.' She gathered her courage. 'And you know
when you said that thing about not wanting to go
into research – like your dad . . . You see . . .' She
struggled to a stop.

Simon said hesitantly, 'You mean when I said finding out how to stop disease was boring?'

'Yeah. My mum died of cancer.' It was still so hard
to say the word.

'I'm so sorry.' He looked cross with himself. 'I've
said a lot of stuff without thinking about it.'

'No, you weren't to know. I should have said at the time . . .' She lifted her gaze. 'Anyway, I'm sorry. Again.'

'Me too.'

They looked at each other and for an absurd moment, Kate felt as though she wanted to step forward into his arms. But almost as the thought slid into her head, she blushed fiercely and turned away. *What on earth made you think of that?* she scolded herself.

'Oh, good, it's you two.' Janet came into the shop and spotted them. 'Excellent – Kate, we've sold nearly all your plants on the *Flowers Say It All* display, can you do us some more?'

'All of them?' Kate was grateful for the diversion and hoped her face would return to its normal colour soon. 'But there were at least ten there yesterday when I left.'

'I know,' said Janet, beaming, 'but someone came in very early this morning and bought most of them. He said he'd got a big family get-together this afternoon and had been sent out to get presents for everyone. He was thrilled with the plants, said it meant he could get something special for all the aunts and uncles.' Her smile grew even wider. 'And it turns out he's a radio presenter on Parchester FM and he said he'd mention us on his show tomorrow morning!'

'What!'

'I know! So we need to make sure we've got lots of plants out for people to buy. Isn't it brilliant? You're such a clever girl!'

Kate glanced instinctively towards Simon and was startled to catch him looking back at her. She turned away quickly. *Oh no, I'm blushing again!* 'That's great, Janet. I'll get going on them now. But . . . I'll need Simon.' She stopped to clear her throat which was suddenly making her voice go squeaky. 'I'll need Simon to do the labels like last time.'

'Of course,' he said immediately. 'As long as you didn't want me to do something else, Janet.'

'No, no, you go and help Kate.' Janet smiled at him. 'A lot of people have commented on the handmade labels. I didn't know you could do such lovely calligraphy, Simon.'

Now it was Simon's turn to blush! Kate felt secretly pleased. 'We'll do as many as we can,' she told Janet.

'Excellent. And the banner has arrived early, too, so maybe you could put that up when you've got a minute. It's in the staff room.'

Kate was glad to be busy again. That odd moment with Simon had been a bit unsettling. What had made her want to hug him? It wasn't like her at all! She quickly found her list of plants for the *Flowers Say It All* range and began collecting them from the various parts of the centre, ready for potting up in the shiny ceramic bowls. Simon squeezed himself into the staff room, since the ground outside was still wet with rain, and began carefully writing new labels.

When Kate came to find him half an hour later, he had already done six labels. 'These are lovely,' she said. 'I think they're even better than the ones you did last week.'

Simon grinned. 'Just don't tell anyone I did them. If the boys at school heard I was doing fancy writing and using glitter, they'd never let me hear the end of it.'

Kate gave a laugh. 'I suppose it's not really a boy thing, doing arts and crafts.'

'No, I'm supposed to be playing rugby or football.' Simon made a comical face. 'At least gardening is a tough job – all that digging and lifting. It's macho enough.'

'Yeah,' said Kate, unable to resist, 'it's not a girl's thing, is it? I mean, girls are more into pretty flowers . . .'

Simon rolled his eyes. 'I *knew* you'd bring that up! Look, I'm sorry if I was rude that first day. I guess

I was nervous. And Janet didn't help, telling me you came here with your granddad all the time and knew everything there was to know about the centre.'

'She said that?' Kate was surprised. 'But that's not true. I come here with Anpa sometimes but he mostly comes on his own.'

'Anpa? Why do you call him that?'

'Oh . . .' Kate was embarrassed. 'It's what I used to call him when I was little and couldn't say grandpa. It sort of stuck.'

Simon was grinning again. 'It's not as bad as what we called our grandma – Ya Ya.'

'*Ya Ya?* Where did that come from?'

'Oh, it's just a nickname.' Simon reached for a pot of glitter. 'You can imagine what kind of teasing I got at primary school though when she came to pick me up one day.' The lid came off with a jerk and spilled glitter all over the little table. 'Oh no.'

'Whoops. Here, I'll help.' Kate leaned forward to scoop up some of the glitter just as Simon did the same from the other side of the table. Their hands brushed together and both of them jumped backwards as though they'd been burned. 'Oh, sorry!' said Kate.

'No, no, it was my fault.'

'Um, I'm just going to . . .' Kate escaped hurriedly from the room, her hand tingling where it had brushed against Simon's. *What on earth is going on?* Her head felt as though it were full of bees, buzzing around. *So you touched his hand – what's the big deal? Good grief, next thing you know you won't even be able to LOOK at him!*

♥

Kate busied herself with planting up the flowers in their new pots, but after an hour even she had to acknowledge that she had to go back and collect the labels from Simon. *Stop being silly*, she told herself, as she headed back to the staff room, her heart thumping more loudly than usual. *You're only going to ask him for the labels, for goodness' sake!*

Simon straightened up slowly. 'Ow,' he said. 'I think my back's got stiff.'

'How are you getting on?' asked Kate. 'Have you got some more labels?'

Simon pointed to a pile, perched precariously on the top of the filing cabinet. 'There you go. I wasn't sure how many crocosmia we had, so I only did two.'

Kate picked up the bright green 'Good Luck!'

labels that were to be tied to the crocosmia plants. 'They're lovely. I think I've got five crocosmia though, so we could do with three more labels.'

'I'll do them in a bit,' said Simon. 'I need to stand up. Why don't I come and help you tie on the labels? Oh – and we need to put the banner up too – I've found the tube it's in.'

Together, they headed out to the nursery. 'It's drying out at last,' commented Simon. 'About time.'

'Yes, but the plants look so much better for all that rain. Everything looks kind of shiny and new.' Kate stopped, thinking to herself, *You idiot! What a dumb thing to say!*

But Simon was nodding. 'Like it's been freshly painted.'

A warmth swept through Kate, and it was nothing to do with the sun. 'Here we are,' she said quickly. 'If you take the ones this end, I'll start at the other end. I've cut the ribbon lengths ready.'

For a few minutes there was silence as they worked. 'How did you come up with these anyway?' Simon asked. 'I mean, I know you said you were thinking about people buying gifts, but what made you think of using the language of flowers?'

'It'll sound silly,' said Kate reluctantly.

He looked interested. 'I won't laugh.'

'It wasn't really my idea.' She couldn't meet his eye. *Why don't you just say you don't remember?* 'It was my mum's.'

'Your mum's? But I thought you said—'

'Yeah,' she broke in hurriedly. 'That's right. But she used the language of flowers all the time in her work. And I'd been reading some of her books. I just hadn't put two and two together until – until I asked her for help. And when I woke up, I had the idea. It was just there, in my head.'

Simon was listening intently.

Don't tell him about the lily smell, he'll think you're crazy. 'And I could – smell lilies. They were her favourite flower. Beauty and purity.' *Great, just great – well done, Kate, you've just made him think you are completely delusional.* She squinted sideways at him. 'I told you it was silly.'

Simon shook his head slowly. 'No, it's not silly. It's kind of cool. Weird though, about the lily smell. And there weren't any lilies in the room?'

'No.'

'Stuff like that is impossible to explain,' he mused. 'Random.' He looked up at her again.

'Yeah . . .' His eyes were *very* dark brown, weren't they? She'd never seen eyes that dark before. And she'd never noticed what dark eyelashes he had either – was that normal for a boy?

'You've got some dirt . . .' Simon indicated a place on his own cheek.

'What?' Kate rubbed her face. 'Is that it?'

'No, it's further over.' He reached across. 'Here.' He touched her cheek gently, but instead of pulling away, he seemed frozen in that position, one fingertip resting against her cheek, his eyes locked on hers.

Kate almost forgot to breathe. Her cheek tingled as though stung by a nettle.

'Hello?' A vaguely familiar voice called out, startlingly close. 'Anyone here?'

Simon sprang back, his face colouring under his tan.

Kate wiped her cheek hastily and scrambled to her feet, her heart racing. 'Hello? Uh – hang on a minute.'

A girl appeared in the greenhouse doorway. 'Hi there, I hope it's OK to come in. I asked the lady on the desk where you were, Kate, since you'd been so helpful the other day.' She grinned. 'I said I wanted personal customer service from the best assistant in the centre.' Her grin widened. 'I think she thought I was taking the mickey to start with, but luckily I remembered your name! She said I could go into the nursery just this once – it's nice in here, isn't it?' She seemed to realize the others hadn't said anything yet. 'Everything OK?'

'Um,' said Kate, her mind fizzing. 'Uh – Libby?'

Libby looked surprised. 'Of course it's me! My mum's sent me with yet another unreadable list. I need you to help me.' She stuck her hand out towards Simon. 'Hello, I'm Libby.'

'Oh – hi.'

'You're Simon, aren't you?'

He looked taken aback. 'Yes. How did you . . .'

But Libby had noticed the plants. 'Wow, these look fab. I love the ribbons. What are they for?'

'We've got a new display,' Kate said, still trying to drag her brain together. It seemed to be floating around her head in tiny pieces. 'It's called *Flowers Say It All*. It's about the language of flowers – you know, each flower has a meaning?'

'Does it? Wow, that's kind of cool.' Libby reached for a label on a rose. '*You Are Beautiful,*' she read out, and then looked straight at Simon. 'That's sweet.'

'That's what a burgundy rose means,' said Kate firmly. *Is she flirting with Simon?* 'But don't ever send a yellow one – it means *jealousy*.'

'Oh.' Libby glanced from one to the other, finally

registering that maybe something was going on. 'Well, I'll keep an eye out for them. I'm sure my mum would love something like this.' She smiled brightly. 'I was wondering if you could give me a hand, Kate. Mum's suddenly obsessed with building a rock garden. I haven't the faintest idea what half the things on this list are. Would you mind?' She held up a scribbled piece of paper.

'I'll find them,' said Kate, wishing that Libby hadn't chosen this day, this moment, to show up. But there wasn't anything she could do about it. 'See you in a bit,' she said to Simon.

'Bye, Simon.'

'Yeah, bye, um – Libby.'

Kate felt a tiny glow of satisfaction that Simon didn't seem the least bit interested in Libby. *But why should you care?* the tiny voice whispered. *It's not as though you're interested in him yourself – is it?*

Libby grabbed Kate's arm as they walked back to the sales area. 'He is simply to *die* for! You must be in heaven working with him every day!'

'Um . . .'

'Those eyes! And that skin! Have you found out if he's Spanish? I bet he is – or Mexican or something.' For a moment she looked disappointed. 'It's a shame he doesn't have an accent. But I suppose he's properly

English, you know – been brought up here and all that.'

Kate felt bewildered. Libby's mouth didn't seem connected to her brain at times – it was almost as though it was just running by itself. And the way she was talking to Kate, as though they were old friends – it was a bit odd. Kate wasn't sure what to say. She didn't think she'd ever met anyone like Libby before. Megan had a friend called Mari who was very outgoing too, but Kate had only met her once when she went to watch Megan in a dance competition. And Mari had been more excited about Megan's dancing than about the boys that were around. Whereas Libby had admitted herself she was completely boy-obsessed!

'Where's that list again?' Kate asked eventually.

Libby clapped a hand to her head dramatically. 'I'm so sorry, what an idiot I am! Here you are. A cute boy makes me go all silly. I'm not like this *all* the time, I promise.' She grinned. 'I'm just jealous, that's all.'

'Of me?' Kate was genuinely surprised.

'Yes, working with Simon. You get to look at him every day!'

'I guess so.' Kate's forehead creased. 'I don't really – um – see him like that though.'

Libby stared. 'What? You mean you haven't noticed how utterly drop-dead gorgeous he is? Really?'

'Well . . .' Kate felt as though Libby were somehow peeling back the layers of shyness she had built around herself. 'I mean, I suppose he has got nice eyes . . .'

'Is he going out with anyone?' asked Libby.

Kate shook her head. 'I don't know, sorry. We haven't talked about – uh, that kind of thing.'

Libby grinned again. 'It would have been the first thing I'd have asked. I don't suppose you'd give him my phone number, would you?'

Kate's jaw dropped. 'Oh! Um . . . I suppose I could.' Her face flushed as she imagined Simon unfolding the piece of paper, reaching for the phone, dialling Libby's number . . . what would he say? *Hi, I noticed you looking at me. You want to go out sometime?* Her imagination gave up. She hadn't been on a date; she didn't know how it worked. Had Simon been on dates?

Libby's gaze sharpened. 'Uh-oh. Wait just one tiny second.' She pulled Kate into a customer-free corner. 'You *like* him, don't you? It's OK, you can tell me. I don't want to tread on anyone's toes.'

'No, it's not . . .' Kate felt profoundly uncomfortable.

'It's OK,' Libby said again, her voice suddenly gentle. 'You're shy. You don't know how to make a move.'

'I haven't had a boyfriend,' mumbled Kate in confusion. *Make a move?* Good grief, no! She didn't want to do that! Or did she? Her head filled with whirling agitation.

Libby nodded slowly. Subtly her attitude had changed. Now she was a confidante, a counsellor – someone to help and give advice. 'Do you want me to give you a few pointers? Because boys need them, you know. If you want to go out with him, he won't notice unless you make it obvious.'

'I don't know if I want to go out with him . . .'

Libby shrugged, grinning. 'What's not to like? He's into plants, you're into plants. He's gorgeous. You're cute. It's a match made in heaven.'

Kate pushed a hand through her hair, embarrassed. 'I'm not cute.'

'Yes you are. You've got freckles and curly hair. Trust me. Now,' said Libby, sounding more practical, 'I won't give him my phone number, obviously. Not if you want to ask him out first.' She grinned.

'I can't ask him out.'

'Course you can. You just need a bit more confidence. Or if you can't do it face-to-face, send him a text or write him a note or something. I once spelled out CALL ME to a boy using pasta shells. I left it on his desk at school.'

'Oh! How – um, did it work?'

'You bet it did!' Libby grinned. Then her face fell. 'Of course, that was before I realized he was still secretly seeing his old girlfriend. But then I should have known it wouldn't work. We had nothing in common. You've got to like the same things, haven't you? That's what all the magazines say.' She broke off. 'Which is why you should definitely go out with Simon. If you want to, I mean . . . Course, if you *don't* want to, *please* let me know! I could develop an interest in gardening like *that*!'

♥

That night, Kate missed her mum so much it made her curl up into a ball and hide under the duvet. *If you were here*, she thought, *I could have asked your advice about boys. I could have told you about Simon and how I don't know if I fancy him or not. You would have understood. We could have had mother–daughter chats about boyfriends and kissing and dating. I can't ask Dad or Anpa – they've never been a teenage girl, they don't know what it's like.*

She could ask Megan, of course, when she came back from holiday. But Megan seemed so sorted about that kind of thing. She and Jake were made for each other (common interests, Libby would say) and Kate shied away from asking too much about relationship things. It was a different world, and she wasn't sure she was ready yet.

Or was she? It was true that since that moment in the greenhouse when he'd touched her cheek, she'd hardly been able to stop thinking about it. Had he been about to kiss her? (Did she even *want* him to kiss her?) Or was it just one of those weird moments that never happened again? Did she *want* it to happen again? It had been exciting but kind of terrifying too. Kate sighed. It was all so confusing!

Maybe Megan would understand? After all, she'd made a boyfriend mistake herself last year, she'd told Kate. She'd been besotted with a boy she thought was fantastic – sensitive, exciting, charming. But he hadn't turned out to be as nice as she'd thought, and then she'd realized that actually her perfect boyfriend had been right under her nose all the time – her best friend, Jake.

Kate turned over in bed and squeezed her eyes shut. It was all so hard. Friends were good – friends could be *great* – but they weren't a mum. There were times that only a mum would do. And she'd never have that again.

Why did you have to die? Kate thought fiercely into her pillow. *Why now, when I'm not ready for you to go, when I still need to ask you things?*

And what am I going to do about Simon?

♥

In the morning, there was again a faint scent of lilies in the air. Kate woke with a new sense of calm. *It's going to be all right*, her mother seemed to be saying. *Don't worry. Things will turn out fine, you'll see.*

But when she arrived at Tilworths, there were three police cars parked outside.

Chapter 9

Judas Tree

'I'm sorry, you can't come in,' said the uniformed officer at the front. He frowned at her. 'The store is closed today.'

'But I work here,' said Kate.

His eyes narrowed. 'That's different, then. You'd better come over here.' He led her through the double doors. There were uniformed and non-uniformed police officers standing around, comparing notes, barking orders to each other and speaking on radios. To her left, Kate caught sight of Janet standing with Carol and Polly. She was shocked by Janet's appearance. The woman seemed to have aged about twenty years since yesterday. Her red, swollen eyes stood out sharply in her white face.

Kate wanted to ask the policeman what had happened, but she didn't dare. Luckily, Janet had spotted her and was coming over, her hands held out in front of her. 'Kate, sweetheart, I'm so sorry about all this. You won't be able to work here today.'

'What's going on?'

Janet took her hands, and her voice shook. 'There's been some – vandalism, I suppose you'd call it.'

'Like last time?'

'Much, much worse.' Janet took a breath. 'Someone got in last night and destroyed most of our stock.'

Kate glanced around the shop. Everything looked just as normal in here.

'No, not here,' Janet said, following her gaze. 'Outside. The plants.' She swallowed. 'They've killed the plants.'

Kate felt her heart give a stuttering thump. '*What? But – but how?*'

Janet addressed the plain-clothes officer behind Kate. 'I'm showing her the damage.'

The officer opened her mouth, but Janet forestalled her. 'We'll stand in the doorway,' she said firmly. 'We won't touch anything.'

The officer glanced at Kate, shrugged and turned away.

'Just a load of plants to them,' muttered Janet fiercely as she pulled Kate to the automatic doors. 'They don't *care*. Not like we do.'

'Janet . . .'

'Look. *That's* what they've done.' Janet swore under her breath. 'You see?'

Kate did see. Her jaw dropped. The shelves, usually bursting with greenery, were full of brown leaves. Plants drooped, flowers had withered and some plastic pots looked as though they had melted. 'Do Not Cross' tape stretched around the whole area. Two people in white paper suits were examining a shelf together and placing tiny fragments in plastic bags. The place looked like it had suffered the worst drought in history, and yet Kate knew those plants had been bursting with life only the day before. 'What happened?' she whispered, when she could find her voice.

'Caustic soda,' said Janet bitterly. 'Sprayed on the plants. That's what they think, anyway. You mustn't touch anything; it's very dangerous.'

'Caustic soda?' Kate couldn't take it in. 'Isn't that what people use to clean their drains? Someone sprayed it on the plants? But – but why?'

Janet shook her head, and her eyes filled with tears. 'I don't know,' she said. 'I don't know, I don't know.'

Polly appeared behind Janet, her usually cheerful round face creased with worry. 'Come on, Janet. Don't stand looking at it. It just makes things worse.'

'Worse?' Janet gave a harsh-sounding laugh. 'It

couldn't *be* worse. This is the end, Polly, you know it is.'

'Nonsense,' said Polly robustly. 'What about all the plants in the nursery? They haven't been touched. And you've got insurance for this, haven't you?'

'What's the point?' Janet said dully as Polly led her away. 'What's the point of fighting? I can't do it any more, Polly.'

Kate didn't hear what Polly said next because at that moment she saw Simon coming in through the main doors. Her heart thumped. Suddenly, she wanted to be the one to tell him. 'Simon! Over here.'

He came over, his expression puzzled and wary. 'What's going on? Why are the police here?'

'Come with me. You have to see this.' Kate took him over to the automatic doors where she had been standing with Janet. 'Someone broke in last night and sprayed caustic soda on all the plants.' Now that she was saying the words, Kate felt a wave of sadness wash over her. She loved these plants; had spent many hours looking after them. And now someone had just come in and killed them all. She felt tears prick her eyes. She suddenly remembered the *Flowers Say It All* display and felt sick. Had it escaped the damage? It was under cover, but it was part of the outside area, even so . . .

Simon stared out at the devastation. 'What the . . . *caustic soda?*' His face went white. 'Are you *sure?*' He took a step forward, and instantly the plain-clothes officer appeared at his side.

'Don't go out there please, young man. No one's to touch anything. You two shouldn't even be standing here.'

'We work here,' murmured Simon, still staring at the dead and dying plants.

'I know that, but this is a crime scene now. You should go and sit somewhere indoors.'

'Maybe we should go home,' Kate tentatively suggested. 'Rather than get in the way.'

The woman shook her head. 'Sorry, I'll need to talk to you both later this morning. Take statements from you.'

Simon's head snapped round. 'Statements? From us? Why?'

The woman's gaze sharpened. 'Because you work here and your evidence could be useful.' She stared from one to the other for a moment and Kate felt as if she were being scanned from head to toe, checking for criminal thoughts. It made her uncomfortable. 'Go and sit with the others in the gift section, please. We'll be taking statements all morning and gathering evidence. Just don't go outside and don't touch anything.'

Simon glanced at Kate, and she could almost guess

what he was thinking: *Who could do something like this?* His dark eyes were worried, and without thinking, Kate held out her hand to him. But he was turning away and didn't see it. *Quick, pull it back!* Kate felt her face flush red – why had she reached for his hand? Thank goodness nobody had noticed! Trying to compose herself, she followed him back into the shop and over to where Janet, Polly and Carol were sitting on garden furniture. Polly patted a chair next to her. 'Come and sit down, you two. It's a big shock for everyone, I know.'

Squashing the faint feeling of disappointment that Simon hadn't held her hand, Kate saw the expressions of despair on the faces of the others. 'I can't believe it,' she said. 'Who would do such a thing?'

'Sick people,' said Carol vehemently. 'People who like seeing others suffer.'

There was a silence. No one seemed to know what to say to this. Janet stared at the ground, her face fixed in a permanent expression of shock. Carol patted her back once or twice but then realized it wasn't being appreciated, so withdrew her hand and gazed at the shelves. Polly sighed every two minutes.

Kate could hardly bear to ask, but she had to know. 'The *Flowers Say It All* display . . .' she said timidly. 'Was it . . . ?'

Polly nodded, her eyes sympathetic. 'I'm so sorry, Kate. Those too.'

'Oh.' Kate swallowed. They'd put out a whole new display yesterday evening! All those hours of work . . . Her eyes filled with tears and she tried to wipe them away quickly. It wasn't fair to get upset in front of the others. They had worked here even longer than she had. She glanced at Simon, wanting to share her disappointment with him, but was startled by his expression. His eyes were restless, darting around the centre, resting on a police officer here, a door there. His fingers twisted themselves together. Every now and then, he frowned and looked down at the floor, as though he were trying to work out a difficult problem.

What is he thinking about? she wondered.

♥

It was a long morning. Kate didn't know what to say to Janet, who looked as though her life were falling apart in front of her eyes. When Mike came in from talking to one of the detectives, he looked much the same. 'They want all our paperwork too,' he told Janet, not caring who heard. 'They've taken the filing cabinets. Just in case there's someone who has a grudge against us.' He snorted. 'I told them good luck since they've still got twenty years' worth of stuff in them.'

Janet barely took this in. 'Grudge?' she repeated, bewildered. 'Grudge?'

Mike gave a tired shrug. 'They say it was carefully planned. Not a spontaneous thing, not like the other stuff.'

'Why do they think that?' asked Simon, and his voice sounded tense.

'The bolt on the front gate was cut,' said Mike. 'You'd need heavy-duty cutters to do that. Not the sort of thing people carry around. Anyone can pick up a brick and throw it through a window, but they say this was different. Then there's the caustic soda, of course . . .' His face crumpled as he said the words, and Kate knew exactly how he felt – all those beautiful plants, destroyed by a quick spray of a deadly substance. 'Someone brought spray canisters of it, and they'd have needed protective clothing.'

'So they don't think this is linked to the stealing and the graffiti?' asked Polly.

Mike shrugged. 'They're not ruling it out, but it seems unlikely.'

'Where would someone get caustic soda?' asked Kate. 'If it's that dangerous?'

Mike shrugged. 'You can buy it at most DIY stores.

People don't realize how toxic it is. That stuff eats through anything, even skin.'

Kate shivered. Polly turned to her, concerned. 'It's all right, Kate. Nobody got hurt. And they didn't get the plants in the nursery either.'

Mike frowned and sat down with them. 'It's odd, that. If they cut through the bolt on the front gate, they could have cut through the nursery bolt. They could have wiped out everything in there too. It's almost as though they wanted to hurt us but not destroy us. Show us they could do worse if they liked.' His mouth twisted. 'Rubbing salt into the wound.'

Take almost everything away . . . but not quite. Kate felt cold. What an awful, mean thing to do to someone. Leave them with a little hope, making it even harder to keep going.

Janet let out a sound that was half sob, half snort.

Mike turned to her. 'I'm so sorry, my love.' He put his arms around her. 'Maybe it's not as bad as we think. We need to take an inventory as soon as we can. And Polly's right – nobody got hurt, that's the main thing.'

'*I'm* hurt,' mumbled Janet into his shoulder. 'They may not have sprayed me with chemicals but it feels just as bad. We can't survive this, Mike.' She gulped.

'All the little things recently, and now this . . . I can't do it any more. We'll have to sell up.'

Kate felt a sharp pain in her stomach, like something breaking. She felt so sorry for Janet and Mike that she thought she might cry again, so got up quickly, mumbling about needing the toilet. She went through to the staff area and shut the door behind her before the tears spilled from her eyes. It was all so awful, and Janet and Mike looked as though they were crumbling away with sadness. She rested her head against the staff-room door and squeezed her eyes tightly closed, trying to keep as quiet as she could.

'Are you all right?'

Simon had followed her through to the corridor. He put a hand on her shoulder. 'Kate?'

She tried to speak, to say she was all right, but her lip wobbled, and she clamped her mouth shut in case she burst out crying again. Instead she shrugged, trying to convey by some kind of sign language that everything was fine really; he shouldn't worry about her.

Simon hesitated for a moment and then put both arms around her, hugging her tightly. He smelled of mint soap and the outdoors. Kate stopped breathing for a moment. *He's hugging me! Simon is actually holding me!* She buried her face in his shoulder, grateful that he couldn't see that her cheeks had instantly flamed scarlet. *This is way better than holding his hand . . . oh, everything's so complicated!* She had been feeling so upset and worried about the attack on the centre, and now here she was feeling something entirely different in Simon's arms!

What am I feeling exactly? Kate wondered in a fuzzy way. All she was sure of was that it was a nice place to be . . .

Simon pulled away. 'Sorry,' he said awkwardly. 'I know how you're feeling.'

Does he?

'About the flower display,' he went on.

Oh . . .

'You put so much work into it.'

'So did you,' Kate replied, hastily wiping her eyes and hoping she wasn't blushing any more.

'Yes, but it was your idea, and your mum and everything . . .' He left the words hanging. There was a pause, and then he cleared his throat. 'Anyway, I just wanted to . . . er . . . don't you think it's a bit strange?'

'What?'

'All this, just after—'

The door opened again and Polly came into the

corridor. 'Kate, are you all right? I know it's been a bit of a shock. I'm sorry you two have to be here – Janet's been trying to persuade the inspector to let you go home.'

'No, no, it's fine,' said Kate, wondering what Simon had been about to say. What did he mean, 'it's a bit strange'? 'We were just coming back.'

Janet and Carol were no longer there, so only Mike sat silently staring at the floor. 'Listen, Mike,' said Polly, as she and Simon and Kate joined him, 'we've got a delivery coming today, shall I ring them and put it off?'

Mike blinked, as though bringing himself back to reality. 'Yes. That's a good idea, Polly, thanks. And I suppose we'd better call Jason and Bob and ask them to come in specially. I don't like to do that on their days off, but this is a bit different.'

'Bob's at a funeral,' Polly told him, 'but I can leave a message. I'm sure he can give a statement another time.'

Mike nodded and Polly headed off. 'I need to have another look round the nursery,' he said to no one in particular. 'Make some notes about which plants need to be potted up for sale as quickly as possible. I don't know how long the police will need to keep this closed, but I guess the shelves will all have to be decontaminated or something too. Possibly we'll have to burn them all. There's going to be a lot of work to do. No point making decisions about our future right now.' He walked slowly away, feeling in his pockets for a pen and notepad.

As Mike disappeared round the corner, the plain-clothes detective who had spoken to Kate and Simon earlier arrived from another direction. 'Hi,' she said, sitting down without preamble. 'I'm Detective Sergeant Kemmitt and I'm in charge of this investigation. You two are here on summer jobs, is that right?'

'Yes,' said Kate.

'Right,' said DS Kemmitt. She waved an arm at another man standing close by. 'This is Detective Constable Ferrers and he'll be taking some notes. We'll need you to give full statements in a bit, where we'll take our time and write them all out fully, but for the moment I could do with just asking a few questions.' She shot a look at DC Ferrers, who hurriedly stepped forward with his notepad. DS Kemmitt took a quick glance at it. 'That's right. So you two are Kate Morrell and Anatoli Ballios, is that right?'

Kate blinked. 'Who? No, this is Simon.'

'We have you down as Anatoli,' DS Kemmitt said to Simon.

He hesitated for a moment and Kate saw his eyes

flick momentarily in her own direction. 'Yes, that's me,' he said, and the world spun. A coldness started at her feet and crept up her legs. She couldn't have stood up if she'd tried.

Anatoli Ballios? But his name is Simon! she repeated dully in her head. *What are they talking about? Why did he say his name was Simon if it isn't?*

Kate tried to concentrate on what DS Kemmitt was saying, but her mind was on repeat. *Anatoli . . . Simon . . . Anatoli . . . Simon . . .* It wasn't just the first name either. Something else was nagging at her, something to do with his surname. What did the detective say it was again? She answered the questions automatically – they were easy enough – and DS Kemmitt gave the impression she was satisfied with their answers.

'Right,' said DS Kemmitt after a while, 'that all seems straightforward. Kate, if you go with DC Ferrers now, he'll go through everything in more detail and write it up for you. We'll bring the statement in tomorrow for you to read through and sign. Anatoli, if you wouldn't mind waiting here until Kate's finished, then she can go home.'

'All right,' Simon said. He was looking at Kate, something curious in his gaze, as though he wanted to tell her a whole lot more but couldn't. She felt as though her own agonized thoughts must be burning their way to him in return. *Who are you? What's your real name?* And, more than anything, *Why did you put your arms around me back in the corridor?* Suddenly there were more questions than she could bear, but there was no opportunity to talk now. She had no choice but to get up and follow the constable.

DS Kemmitt's expression softened slightly. 'The sooner we're done here, the sooner you can go home.' She almost looked sympathetic as Kate turned away.

But Kate was buried under the mountain of words and memories. *Anatoli . . . Simon . . . big family . . . touched my cheek . . . told me I was clever . . . listened to me . . . looked at me with those amazing dark eyes . . . don't you think it's a bit strange?*

That elusive thing was tugging at her brain again, what was it? Something to do with a name . . . but why did she have the feeling it was also to do with a conversation she'd had a while ago? *Think, think!*

And under it all was the awful swirling gut-wrenching anxiety . . . *Simon lied to me. And I was just starting to think that maybe . . . maybe I liked him a lot. More than I've liked any boy. But he's not who I thought he was. If he's lied about his name . . . how can I believe anything he says?*

Chapter 10

Scotch Thistle

Anpa stared at her in horror. 'Someone did *what?*'

'Sprayed caustic soda over the plants,' Kate repeated dully. 'They're all dead.'

Anpa stood as though frozen to the spot.

'Can I come in?' asked Kate. She was still standing on the front doorstep, key in hand. Her grandfather had seen her walking up and got there first, enquiring anxiously why she was home early from work.

Anpa blinked. 'Sorry, love. Of course. You could probably do with a cup of tea too. I'll put the kettle on.'

'I'd prefer squash,' Kate called after him, but Anpa showed no sign he had heard. She sighed and followed him through to the kitchen. Her legs felt like lead. Each step was an effort. It was past two o'clock and she still hadn't eaten any lunch, but she wasn't hungry. She pulled out her packet of sandwiches and sat down at the kitchen table.

Anpa was gazing at the kettle in bewilderment. 'I can't believe it. Why would anyone do such a thing?'

'I don't know.' Kate stared at her sandwich, feeling no desire to eat it. She couldn't stop thinking about Simon. Maybe – Kate's brain whirled rapidly – maybe everything he'd ever said was a lie. When he said his name was Simon, it was a lie. Maybe when he'd said she was clever for coming up with such a good idea, he didn't mean that either. And when he touched her cheek and looked into her eyes . . . maybe that had all been pretend too. Something in her ached at the thought. She felt so tired, and still the questions buzzed around her head. It was like being in a wasps' nest.

'Are the police there? Surely they've called the police.'

'Yes, that's what I've been doing – talking to them.'

'You?' Anpa swung round. 'Why did they want to talk to you?'

'They're talking to everyone who works there, Anpa,' said Kate. 'Whether we've seen anyone suspicious, all that kind of thing. Just like on the TV. And I had to give a statement.' She shrugged. 'I don't think I was very useful though. The policeman looked a bit disappointed when we went through it together.'

'They should have rung your father,' Anpa said, frowning. 'You're a minor, they shouldn't talk to you without an adult present.'

'They brought Polly,' Kate told him. 'I said it didn't matter who was there with me. I didn't want to bother Dad. And there wasn't anything I could tell them anyway.' Had Simon lied to the police? Was Anatoli really his name or was that yet another untruth? Lie upon lie . . . Kate wanted to put her head down on the table and close her eyes in the hope that it would all go away.

Anpa sat down with a thump. 'Poor Mike and Janet.' He shook his head. 'How much stock was destroyed?'

'All the plants that were outside for sale,' said Kate, and her voice wobbled. 'Including my flowers.'

'Oh, Kate. I'm so sorry.' He sighed. 'Well, one thing's for sure. That property developer you were talking about will have a big smile on his face today. Janet and Mike may well be forced to take his offer after this.'

Kate felt as though she had suddenly walked into a brick wall. She actually reeled in shock. *No! But it can't be!* She gripped the table for balance and felt a wave of nausea break over her.

'Kate? You all right?'

For a moment, she couldn't speak. *That's what was nagging at my mind! That name! Ballios, wasn't it? Anatoli Ballios, they called Simon. And . . . Dimitri Ballios, the property developer! They're related!* She closed her eyes and went pale as the world spun.

Anpa's hand closed around her arm. 'Put your head down,' he said firmly. 'You look like you're about to faint. It's all been a bit much, this morning.'

'It's not that,' whispered Kate, her cheek pressed to the cool surface of the table. Should she tell him? But Anpa was her best friend, in a way . . . he would understand, wouldn't he? 'I just realized something . . . about Simon.'

Slowly, the dizzying feeling subsided as she explained.

'So his surname . . . it's the same as the man who wants to buy Tilworths. The one who made them the offer. Is it . . . do you think it could just be a coincidence?'

'Hmm,' Anpa said eventually. 'That doesn't sound good. It's an unusual surname.'

Kate's heart sank. She wasn't quite sure what she'd been expecting, but she had hoped that perhaps

Anpa would say he was sure Simon didn't have anything to do with it, she was just imagining things – and maybe she'd got the name wrong anyway? 'Do you think it could be his father?' she asked faintly.

Her grandfather knew what she meant. 'I don't know, petal. Could be. Could be. But let's not judge before we know the facts, eh?'

'But Simon lied about his name,' Kate said miserably. 'Why would he do that unless he had something to hide?'

Anpa shrugged. 'Who knows? But there might be a very good reason, Kate. Maybe you should talk to him.' He tapped his fingers on the table. 'I'm ringing your dad. He should be here for you.'

'Don't.' Kate didn't want to take her father away from his work. He wouldn't be pleased, she knew. He was always saying how important and precious his time was. 'I'm all right.'

'Then you can tell him that yourself.' Anpa pressed speed-dial and waited for it to connect. 'Nick? John here. I've got Kate home from work. There's been a break-in at Tilworths.' He listened. 'Yes, some vandalism – very nasty. She's all shaken up.' He held the phone out to Kate. 'You talk to him.'

She took the handset. 'Hi, Dad.'

Her father's voice was concerned. 'Are you all right, Kate? What's going on?'

'The police are there, taking statements. I had to talk to them.'

'To the police? What about?'

She shrugged. 'Just about what time I left yesterday and if I'd seen anyone weird hanging around – that kind of thing.'

'What happened then?'

She told him about the destruction of the plants.

Nick whistled. 'Someone must really have it in for them.'

'I know.' Suddenly, she felt frightened. It was such a hateful thing to do, wasn't it? Such strong feelings . . . and what if the person who did it had actually visited the centre while she'd been there? The police seemed to think it was someone with a personal grudge. Had she seen him (or her) in the centre herself? She went cold at the thought.

'Kate?' Her father sounded worried. 'Are you all right? Should I come home?' He hesitated. 'It's not a very good time . . . got a big contract to finish . . . but if you need me . . .' He waited.

Yes! Kate wanted to say. *Yes, I do need you!* She sighed. 'No, it's all right. I'm OK. You don't need to come back.'

'Are you sure?' He sounded relieved.

'Yeah. Anpa's here, he'll look after me.' She saw her grandfather frown and she knew he was disappointed that Nick wasn't coming home. *But what can I say? I am OK really – just a bit confused and tired. What could Dad do anyway?* 'I'll probably just go to bed.'

'That's a good idea.' Nick was warm and reassuring now. 'I'll be home promptly this evening. I'll cook something really nice, how about that? Sausage and mash – that's good for when you're feeling upset.'

'OK.' Kate gripped the phone miserably. Why couldn't she just say, *Yes, please come home?* And more to the point, why did he need her to say it? Couldn't he just come home because he wanted to be with her? *But he doesn't want to be with you*, the voice whispered. *He'd rather be at work than with you, didn't you hear how relieved he was?*

'See you later then. And get some rest.'

'Yeah, I will. Bye.'

Anpa came over to hug her as she put the phone down. 'You sure you want to go to bed, love? Why not sit on the sofa and watch TV? I'll bring you some tea, or how about hot chocolate?'

His arms were so warm and his voice so comforting that everything just came over her at once and Kate burst into tears.

♥

The centre was closed for two days, and even when it re-opened it was only the gift shop that was allowing customers. The outside area was still cordoned off whilst Mike slowly went through the arduous business of checking all the shelving to make sure it didn't need repairing or replacing.

Kate had been into the centre to sign her statement, but hadn't seen Simon since the horrible day of the attack. There were butterflies in her stomach as she arrived in the morning. She had thought about the coincidence with the surnames almost every minute of the day since she found out. She'd even gone to the library to Google the Ballios name, since the home computer kept crashing. There was a website, and even a Wikipedia entry for Dimitri Ballios, detailing his many property successes over the years, but she could find no reference to Simon, or Anatoli, if that was what he was really called. And yet, it wasn't exactly a common name, was it? The website said Dimitri was Greek, which would explain Simon's Mediterranean colouring and why Libby thought he might be Spanish.

Kate felt baffled. If Simon were indeed related to

Dimitri Ballios, why on earth had Janet and Mike offered him a job? They must have known his real name, surely? Otherwise how would the police have known? Kate still had so many questions, but the only person who could answer them was Simon and she wasn't sure she was brave enough to confront him. *Why did I never ask him about himself before? There must have been so many times when I could have asked about his family or his friends . . . why didn't I?*

There was no sign of Simon when she arrived. Carol smiled at her from behind the shop till. 'Hi, Kate. You're helping me this morning, I hope that's all right. Janet wants to see if you can do some more *Flowers Say It All* pots this afternoon, but they're all too busy sorting out the shelving at the moment.'

Kate was a bit disappointed that she couldn't get on with her display straight away, but she nodded at Carol and tried to look enthusiastic.

Carol soon had her running around doing all sorts of jobs. The shop was crammed with items, from wellies to birdseed, wind chimes to money boxes. At the end of the first hour, Carol called Kate over to the till. 'It's not busy today,' she told her, 'because a lot of people don't realize we've re-opened. I really need to organize a shipment of stuff that came in last week. It's sitting out back, still waiting to be dealt with. I'm

going to put you on the till for a bit.' Seeing Kate's
alarm, she added quickly, 'Don't worry, I'll show you
how it works. And if you have any trouble, just give
me a shout. I won't be far away.'

Kate watched closely as Carol talked her through
the controls of the till. She just hoped she could
remember it all. It was true that the centre wasn't
busy this morning; the news of the attack had been
all over the local news, and many people probably
assumed it was still closed. She hoped she wouldn't
have any customers at all whilst Carol was busy!

For half an hour, it looked like she might get
her wish. But then a tall, imposing-looking woman
headed towards her. She wore an expression that
suggested she thought everyone around her was in
some way inferior, and in her arms she held a large
box. She plonked this on the counter in front of
Kate.

'Does this come in gold?'

'Um . . .' Kate was taken aback. The box appeared
to contain a large silver metallic ball that had no
function apart from to sit in a flower bed and 'reflect
the surrounding beauty'. It had undoubtedly come
from the section Carol referred to as 'tat'. 'This is a
silver one,' Kate said.

The woman tutted. 'I know that. I want to know if

it comes in gold. Everything else in my garden is gold. It needs to match the sundial.'

Kate tried not to react with surprise. This woman had a *gold sundial* in her garden? 'I'm sorry, I don't know.'

'Well, can't you find out?' snapped the woman. 'Honestly, show a bit of initiative.'

Kate flushed. The old Kate would have retorted, she knew; stuck up for herself, and inside she still wanted to do that. But the new Kate was too used to keeping quiet and doing what other people asked. 'I could go and ask Carol,' she mumbled.

'You do that,' said the woman, pulling out a powder compact. Kate noticed it had the name 'Vivienne' picked out in diamanté on the top.

'Gold?' repeated Carol with a frown when Kate asked her. 'No, they only do silver. Most people want silver; it's more reflective. Tell her it doesn't come in any other colours.'

'Well?' asked Vivienne, as Kate headed back.

'Sorry,' said Kate, knowing she sounded nervous, and annoyed with herself for letting this woman get to her. 'Sorry, it only comes in silver.'

Vivienne sighed loudly and stared at the box. 'How annoying. You don't know if they do gold ones at the Parchester West Garden Centre, do you?'

Kate shook her head. 'I've no idea.'

Vivienne sighed again. 'All right, all right. I'll pop into Parchester on my way home and see if they've got one. If they do, I'll bring this one back. Of course, it will add an extra five miles onto my journey.' She glared at Kate as though this was in some way her fault.

'So . . .' asked Kate, 'you do want this one then?'

'Yes, yes.' Vivienne dug around in her bag for her purse. 'Though it's ridiculously overpriced, of course.'

Kate held the gun against the barcode and heard it beep. The price came up on the till – £19.99. 'Nineteen ninety-nine, please,' she said, hoping that Vivienne carried cash . . .

'Here you go,' said Vivienne, holding out a piece of bright pink plastic.

Kate's heart sank. She hoped she could remember how the card reader worked, otherwise it would give Vivienne another excuse to be rude to her. 'Thank you,' she said politely, taking the card and slotting it into the machine. Now, what had Carol said?

'Is there a problem?' asked Vivienne, watching Kate stand undecided for a moment.

'No, no,' said Kate. 'Just trying to remember . . . I don't usually work on the till.' She gave what she hoped was a friendly smile, but Vivienne simply stared coldly back.

'I suppose you're here on work experience,' she said, as though 'work experience' was equivalent to 'swimming in manure'.

'A summer job, actually,' replied Kate, feeling a tiny flicker of resentment deep in her stomach. But Janet had talked about good customer service being the most important thing, so she squashed down her irritation.

Vivienne made a snorting sound. 'Still, I suppose it keeps you off the streets.'

Off the streets? What is she talking about? More in hope than expectation, Kate tapped the buttons on the till and was pleasantly surprised when the credit card machine beeped in recognition. Ha! She *had* remembered how to do it! 'Please enter your PIN,' she said to Vivienne, trying not to sound smug.

Vivienne reached forward with an exquisitely manicured finger and stabbed in the numbers.

The machine beeped again. 'I'm sorry,' said Kate. 'Something went wrong there.'

'What do you mean?' Vivienne leaned over to look. 'Card *declined*? That's ridiculous, there's nothing wrong with the card. It must be your machine.'

I don't think so. Kate felt secret satisfaction that Vivienne wasn't as perfect as she pretended. 'Maybe we could try another card?'

Vivienne made an exasperated noise. 'Have you even done it right? Try it again.'

'Yes, I did it right,' said Kate, a sharp edge creeping into her voice. 'The till says there's something wrong with the card. There's no point trying it again.'

'Perhaps you don't know what you're doing,' suggested Vivienne, her eyes flashing.

'Perhaps you've run out of money,' snapped Kate. Instantly, she clapped a hand to her mouth, shocked. *I shouldn't have said that!*

Vivienne gave a sharp intake of breath. '*Well!* If that's what customer service is like here nowadays, I don't think I'll bother! Give me my card.' She practically snatched it from Kate's hand and gave her a venomous glare. 'No wonder this place is going downhill if they can't even get professional staff these days. You tell your manager from me that he's just lost a customer. I might even write and tell him myself. I shall be shopping at Parchester West from now on.' She stuffed her card back into her purse and stalked out, leaving the box on the counter.

Kate felt awful. How could she have handled it so badly! Janet had told her that the customer was always right; that Tilworths went out of its way to help people. And because of Kate, that woman would take her money elsewhere, and she'd probably tell her friends about it too. Vivienne dressed expensively and had expensive tastes. Tilworths *needed* customers like her. In fact, Vivienne was probably exactly the sort of person to buy from the *Flowers Say It All* range too – and now she wouldn't be coming back!

'Didn't she want it after all?' asked Carol in surprise as Kate went to put the box back on the shelf.

Kate shook her head, her face red with shame.

'Are you all right?' Carol asked, her voice sharpening. 'What happened?'

'Nothing.' Kate didn't look at her. 'I just need a minute.' What would Carol say if she knew that Kate had driven away a customer? The more she thought about it, the worse she felt. Janet and Mike needed all the help they could get – Kate should be encouraging *more* people to come to the centre, not driving them away! Absurdly, she felt like crying. 'Going to the loo,' she said hastily to Carol. 'Back in a sec.'

Carol called after her as she headed towards the staff door, but Kate pretended she didn't hear. Another customer was heading towards the till, so Carol was prevented from following. She just needed a few moments to get herself under control. Then she'd come out and apologize to Carol, explain what a mess she'd made of things . . .

But as she turned into the tiny staff room, Kate stopped dead in the doorway at the sight of Simon sitting in a chair examining his hands. 'You!'

He looked up. His face was pale and tired. 'Oh. Hello.'

For a moment, she was speechless. All the carefully practised questions flew out of her head.

'You all right?' asked Simon, in a slightly strained voice.

'What are *you* doing here?'

He was surprised. 'I'm on a break. Mike sent me in here for a bit.'

'I didn't mean that. I meant . . .' And suddenly all of Kate's confusing feelings, mixed with the guilt she felt over her recent encounter, came pouring out in a jumble of anger, 'I meant, how *dare* you show your face here? After what you've done?'

Simon looked uneasy. 'What are you talking about?'

'Don't pretend you don't know!' Kate cried. 'You lied about your name and everything! You're not really called Simon! You're something to do with that horrible man; the one who wants to buy Tilworths and knock it down and build boring houses. You've got the same name as him! And you lied to me about it and . . .' Emotion burst out of her. 'And I wouldn't be surprised if it was *you* who broke in and destroyed everything!' She clenched her fists, shaking.

Simon stared at her, his face as white as the walls.

Chapter 11

Osier

'You're wrong.'

Kate stared with wide eyes, her hands still clenched tight. Simon's voice cracked with emotion.

'You're wrong,' he repeated, and his gaze burned with intensity. 'How could you think . . . ?' He swallowed and tried again. 'I didn't have anything to do with it. I wouldn't, you must *know* I wouldn't. He's my uncle. Dimitri is my uncle.'

'Your *uncle*?'

Simon twisted his fingers together unhappily. 'We don't get on. He and my dad had a massive argument when my grandma died a few years back. Remember I said we called her Ya Ya? It turned out she'd left all her money to our family – my dad and his children – but nothing for my uncle or his kids.'

'Oh.'

'Yeah.' Simon pulled a face. 'It didn't go down too

well. Uncle Dimitri's been trying to contest the will ever since, so no one can get the money yet. Dad says it's costing everyone a fortune to keep going to court. He says by the time the will is finally sorted out, it won't have been worth it, and he's really mad at Uncle for wasting everyone's time and money.' He looked hard at her. 'I haven't seen Uncle Dimitri for ages. As far as I'm concerned he's nothing to do with me. Honestly.'

Kate didn't know what to say.

'I didn't know anything about Uncle Dimitri trying to buy this place until you told me the other day.' Simon's eyes darkened. 'It's just the sort of thing he would do, too. He loves money. He'll do whatever it takes to get more of it.'

'What about your name?' asked Kate, unwilling to let him off so easily.

'It really is Simon,' he told her. 'Well, it's my middle name. My first name is Anatoli.'

'So why don't you call yourself that?'

'I did,' he said with a half-laugh, 'when I was little. But I got picked on – we lived in a village, and we were the only Greek family. The other kids used to make up rhymes about my name, and I hated it so much that when I moved schools I told everyone my name was Simon. It's an English name as well as a

Greek name, so people just accepted it.' He shrugged. 'I got used to it. Hardly anyone calls me Anatoli now except my parents.'

'Oh, I see.' Kate felt as though the floor had suddenly sunk a few inches. She had been so angry with Simon for lying, but his explanations were so believable. 'Sorry. I – er, well . . .'

'It's OK. I can see how it looked. But I didn't have anything to do with this, I promise. I wouldn't lie to you, Kate.' His eyes met hers, and she was instantly absolutely certain of his sincerity. He looked so upset, and it was a tale of family misery. No wonder he didn't speak to his uncle any more. And if she'd been teased about her name at school, she'd probably have changed it too.

She sat down next to him. 'Janet and Mike . . .' she said hesitantly. 'They knew your real name, right?'

'Yes, of course.' Simon raised his eyebrows. 'I know what you're thinking. Ballios isn't exactly a common name.'

'When I overheard them talking, they said the offer was lower than his previous one.'

'So . . .' Simon frowned, 'he must have made an offer before I came to work here.'

'Do you think they made the connection between you and your uncle?'

'If they did, why did they offer me a job?' Simon shook his head. 'And they've been really nice to me, so they can't think . . . oh, I don't know.'

'Your uncle wants to buy this place, right? Does he know about the break-in?'

Simon shrugged. 'I guess so, it was in the local paper, wasn't it? He's probably got the biggest smile on his face ever. Janet and Mike are in an even worse position now. Which is why—'

'That's what my grandfather said,' Kate interrupted. 'Bet he can force them to take his offer.'

'He might even drop it again. Make them take less money.'

'It's been a really good thing for him, hasn't it?' said Kate thoughtfully. 'I mean, it couldn't have come at a better time, someone breaking in and— Oh!'

Their eyes met, and Simon paled. 'I know what you're thinking,' he said quietly. 'Because I've been wondering the same thing.'

'He didn't . . . Do you think . . .' Kate couldn't speak.

Simon shook his head. 'It *can't* be him. I can't believe it.'

There was a pause. 'What's he like?' asked Kate gently. 'Your uncle?'

Simon bit his lip. 'I don't really know any more.

When I was growing up, he was the perfect jolly uncle. He always bought us great presents, and took us out places. He was a laugh. But when Ya Ya died . . . well, he changed. It was like he needed to make more and more money. He started new projects all over the place. And he turned against us. He said some really nasty things – stuff I'd never imagined he would come out with.' He shrugged. 'I don't feel I know him any more. How would I have any idea if he could do something like this?'

Kate reached out and patted his hands hesitantly. 'It's OK,' she said.

'I feel so bad.' Simon held her hand so she couldn't take it away. 'If it was my uncle, I mean. If he *did* do this . . . I'd feel like it's somehow my fault.'

'It wouldn't be,' Kate told him. She pulled slightly, but Simon was holding her hand tight. His was warm and soft. An unfamiliar nervous tickle began somewhere in the region of her tummy button.

'But he's my uncle. Maybe I should tell Janet and Mike I'm giving up my job.'

'No!' Kate was so taken aback the word came out louder than she intended. 'No, don't do that!' She was becoming more and more distracted by the fact that Simon was holding her hand. He didn't even seem aware of it, but she didn't want to pull away in case that made the whole thing embarrassing. *And*, a tiny voice whispered to her, *it feels really nice*.

Simon sighed. 'Why not? If I stay here, they might carry on wondering. I'd hate it if they thought I was somehow—'

'I'll tell them you didn't have anything to do with it,' said Kate fiercely. 'You shouldn't leave. It's not your fault. And besides, you're – you're a good worker.' *And part of why I like working here is because you're here too*, she realized.

Simon smiled at her. 'Thanks. You're really easy to talk to, you know? I haven't told anyone outside the family about Ya Ya's will. I don't know why I told you. You're a good listener.'

'I'm so sorry I shouted at you.'

'You don't have to apologize again.'

'I know. But I seem to be messing everything up at the moment.' She hesitated. 'I said something to a customer that I shouldn't have.' She explained about Vivienne, her face reddening with shame again as she spoke.

Simon put an awkward arm round her shoulders. 'You were upset. Everyone is. Don't blame yourself.'

Kate leaned towards him. He was so warm and comforting! The strange tickle in her stomach intensified as she put her head on his shoulder. His hand rested against her back, and she felt her eyes closing. If she could just stay here for a while . . .

'There you are!' Janet appeared in the doorway, and Kate and Simon sprang apart, embarrassed. 'Carol said you'd run off and she thought you were upset.' Her sharp eyes flicked from one to the other. 'Are you all right?'

Kate flushed. 'I'm fine. Sorry, I just – I didn't handle a customer very well.'

'You're not the only one.' Janet grimaced. 'I nearly hit someone with a spade a minute ago – completely by accident. Can you imagine what would have happened if I *had* hit him? We'd probably have been sued!' She glanced at Simon. 'You on a break?'

'Yeah.' He looked at his watch. 'Should be getting back about now though.'

Janet nodded. 'Half of that shelving needs replacing, Mike says. He wants to move some of the undamaged shelves around to the front and he could do with another pair of hands.' *Is she speaking to Simon a bit more sharply than usual?* wondered Kate. Abruptly Janet swung away from them. 'If you're OK, Kate, Carol says she's got a nice easy job for you in the shop.' The staff door clicked shut behind her.

Kate glanced at Simon, uncomfortable. 'I'm sure she doesn't think . . .' she started to say.

Simon gave her a crooked smile and shrugged. 'Yeah, yeah. But I bet she's wondering, isn't she? I can't stay here if they're suspicious of me.'

'Can't we do something?' Kate said impulsively.

'What do you mean?'

'I don't know, there must be something. Go to your uncle and ask him straight out if he had something to do with it. Clear your name.' She laughed at the absurdity of the idea.

Simon stared at her, his face serious. 'You think we could do that?'

'Well, I . . .' Kate was about to say, *Of course not, I was joking*, but something inside her sparked into life. Didn't she used to be a daredevil? 'Why not? Does your uncle have an office in Parchester?'

'Yes, just off the high street. I've never been there . . .'

'But you know where it is?'

'Yes . . .' Simon said slowly. 'You think we should go?'

'I think,' said Kate, 'that if we want to help Janet and Mike, we need to find out everything about your uncle that we can. And if he *did* have something to do with this . . . then it's up to us to prove it.'

Chapter 12

Larch

By the end of the day, Kate's triumph at her daring suggestion had eroded into gnawing anxiety. As she and Simon walked to the bus stop, she was within seconds of saying, 'Let's forget the whole thing and go home.' But Simon's face had set with a pale determination and she couldn't bring herself to back out now. They sat silently on the bus, watching the railings, houses and parks slide past the window, and Kate's heart hammered so loudly in her chest she was sure everyone could hear it.

'Two more stops,' Simon said.

Kate just gulped and nodded. *What am I doing here? Why on earth did I suggest this? I should be home by now, helping Anpa get supper ready, telling him how things are going at work.* She was glad she had at least rung Anpa to let him know she would be late, though she wished she hadn't had to make up some lie about working late on the display. Being a detective for real was far more nerve-racking than she'd expected. Simon's leg was pressed against hers on the cramped bus seat, but Kate was too nervous to think about it.

'Here we are,' Simon said, and Kate blinked.

'Already?'

But he was clambering down the steps to the door as the bus shuddered to a halt. 'His office is over there,' he told Kate, pointing.

The two of them stood on the pavement and stared at it. It was an unassuming building. You wouldn't even have known it contained offices if it hadn't been for the little labels by the front door buzzers. *Ballios Enterprises*, it said next to the top one.

'OK,' said Kate, everything inside her gripped by a desire to run away. 'Remember what we agreed?'

Simon nodded. His voice was tense. 'I think it can work. You ready?'

'Yes.' Her voice shook slightly and she cleared her throat. 'Yes,' she said, more firmly. 'Ready.'

Simon reached out and pressed the button.

'You're sure he'll be here?' Kate asked. 'It's past five o'clock.'

Simon opened his mouth to reply but the door buzzed. He glanced at Kate with a shrug and pushed it open.

Ballios Enterprises was on the top floor of the

building, and Kate felt mildly surprised when she saw the shabby sign on the door. She had assumed that Dimitri Ballios could afford the smartest office around, but it didn't look like it.

Simon knocked on the door and a female voice called out, 'Come in!'

It was an ordinary-looking office, with an ordinary-looking lady sitting behind the desk. She had an ordinary-looking computer and ordinary-looking bookshelves. In fact, everything looked so very ordinary that Kate began to wonder if they might perhaps be wrong about Dimitri. This was a respectable business – how could it possibly have anything to do with the caustic-soda attack?

'Can I help you?' The lady looked puzzled. Her hair was going grey but she didn't look old. She had square glasses and a friendly face, and a rather too fussy blouse on.

Simon stepped forward. 'Hi. Yes, I was wondering if Mr Ballios was in today?' Kate marvelled at how steady his voice sounded.

'He's on a conference call at the moment,' said the lady. 'Can I ask what it's about?'

'I'm his nephew,' Simon said.

The lady broke into a smile. 'Well, then I'm very pleased to meet you. What was your name?'

'Anatoli,' said Simon, and Kate blinked, even though it was what they had agreed. It just sounded so odd to hear Simon call himself by his other name!

'And this is . . . ?'

'This is my friend, Kate,' said Simon.

'Hello,' said Kate. She was determined to sound as calm as Simon.

The lady smiled at her. 'It's very nice to meet you. But I'm a bit surprised you've come to the office. Is there something you wanted to talk to your uncle about, Anatoli?'

'Yes,' said Simon boldly. 'I want to talk to him about my grandmother's will.'

He's doing brilliantly, thought Kate in admiration. *Just as we planned.*

'Oh, I see.' The lady clearly didn't see, but she was taken aback. 'Well, um . . . let me see if he's got a spare minute.' She pushed back her chair and went to a door in the far wall, knocking on it before passing through.

Simon looked at Kate. 'So far so good,' he said quietly.

Impulsively, Kate reached for his hand and squeezed it. 'You'll be fine.'

He looked surprised but pleased. 'I've only got to keep him talking. You've got the hard job.'

Kate dropped his hand as the door opened and the lady came back into the room. She still looked puzzled, but smiled at Simon. 'He'd be delighted to see you,' she said, and Kate wondered if that were true.

'Thanks,' said Simon.

'Aren't you going in too?' the lady asked Kate.

Kate shook her head. 'No – er . . . it's a family matter. I just came to keep him company. Is it all right if I wait out here?'

'Of course,' said the lady, smiling at her.

Simon caught Kate's eye as he went through the door, and gave her a surreptitious thumbs-up. Just before the door closed behind him, Kate heard him say, 'Hi, Uncle Dimitri, I hope you don't mind . . .'

The receptionist pointed to a small red chair by the main door. 'Have a seat if you like. Do you know if they'll be long?'

Kate shook her head. 'Not really. Si— uh, Anatoli said it was a bit complicated.'

'Oh, I see. What's your name again?'

'Kate.'

'Kate, that's right. I'm Julie.' She sat back in her chair, clearly happy to chat for a bit. 'I didn't even know Mr Ballios had a nephew.'

'They don't get on,' Kate said confidentially. 'There was a big family argument a few years back.'

'Oh, really?' Julie looked interested. *Good*, thought Kate, *I need her to trust me*. 'What kind of argument? He doesn't talk much about his family, you see.'

'Well . . .' Kate leaned forward and lowered her voice. 'Anatoli's grandma died and left all her money to his side of the family – nothing to Dimitri, I mean Mr Ballios. So he and Anatoli's father have had a massive argument and don't talk to each other any more.'

'Goodness!' breathed Julie, her eyes glued to Kate. 'I had no idea! How awful!'

'Yes,' said Kate, wondering just how far she could push this story, 'and Mr Ballios is still contesting the will, so no one has any money, and . . .' A flash of inspiration came to her, 'and Anatoli's little sister needs an operation and if it's to be done quickly they have to pay for it . . .' She couldn't believe she was making all this up, but Julie was leaning across her desk now, drinking it all in. 'And so Anatoli has come to ask Mr Ballios if he'll drop the court case so that they can get the money for her operation.'

Julie's eyes filled with tears. 'Poor little girl! What a terrible situation to be in.'

Kate's gaze sharpened. 'Do you have children?'

Julie nodded. 'Oh yes, two girls. They're my world. Come round here . . .'

Kate got up and went round the end of Julie's desk. 'There,' said Julie, indicating her computer screen. The wallpaper showed a photograph of two smiling girls, holding ice creams. 'That was taken a couple of weeks ago on the beach,' Julie said fondly.

'It looks lovely, where were you?' Kate shot a look at the filing cabinet standing to her right.

'Majorca,' said Julie with a sigh. 'It was gorgeous. Ever so hot though. The girls had never been abroad before, but Mr Ballios gave me a nice bonus last Christmas—' She broke off hurriedly, colouring. 'Anyway, it makes a change from Cornwall.'

Why is she embarrassed about getting a bonus? wondered Kate. *My dad gets bonuses, they're not exactly a secret . . . unless there was something wrong with the money . . . ?* 'So how long have you been working here?' she asked, perching on the desk.

'Two years,' said Julie. 'It's all right.'

'What's Mr Ballios like?'

Julie frowned, and Kate suddenly felt she'd gone too far. 'I mean, he's Anatoli's uncle,' she added hastily, 'but Anatoli doesn't really know much about him.'

Julie relaxed slightly. 'He's a good boss,' she said, though she sounded a little wary. 'And it's good that he lets me work flexible hours, so that I can be with my girls when they come home from school. Not today,' she went on, seeing Kate glance at the clock. 'They're at ballet until six.'

'Oh, they do ballet?'

'They love it.' Julie beamed. 'All those pink leotards and tights and doing their hair.'

'Ballet's kind of expensive,' Kate said, wondering where this conversation was going and how much time she had left.

'It certainly is,' agreed Julie. 'Good thing I've got a decent job.'

Kate waved an arm at the office. 'It all looks very organized.'

'Oh, it is. Look.' Julie got up and went to the filing cabinet. She pulled out the top drawer. 'I can find anything I need straight away. See – these are the different clients' names and each one has a file. And everything's colour-coded, of course.'

'Wow.' Kate's gaze travelled rapidly across the top of the drawer. Aconite . . . Armstrong . . . Bowler . . . Drum . . . This was just the beginning of the alphabet; the rest must be in the lower drawers. Her heart leaped. She needed to see if there was a file for Tilworths! 'There's a filing cabinet where I work,' she said, 'but it's stuffed full, nowhere as organized as this.'

'Where you *work?*' Julie stared. 'How old are you?'

'Oh, it's a summer job,' said Kate, almost biting her

tongue. Of all the stupid things she could have said! *Don't mention the word Tilworths, whatever you do!* 'It's . . . uh . . . an office.'

'You're too young to be working in an office,' said Julie.

'No, no.' Kate waved a hand, trying to conjure an explanation out of thin air. 'It's my dad's office. I'm just helping him out a bit.'

'Oh, I see.' Julie frowned and glanced at the clock. 'They've been a long time in there.'

'Uh . . . maybe you should go and see if every-thing's all right?' suggested Kate.

Julie hesitated. 'I don't know. He doesn't like me barging in.'

'What time do you have to pick your daughters up from ballet?'

Julie nodded. 'I should be going soon. All right, I'll just stick my head in . . .' She got up from her desk, clicking 'Log Off User' with the mouse. The com-puter screen went blank. Kate didn't mind; it wasn't the computer she was interested in.

Julie knocked softly on the office door. The moment she opened it and stepped inside, Kate was over to the cabinet in a flash and pulling out the bottom drawer as quietly as possible. Surely the letter T would be in here . . . Her heart leaped as she saw the word

TILWORTHS neatly printed on a green file. Hastily, she pulled it out – goodness, it was big! How on earth was she going to hide it?

'All right then,' she heard Julie say, and she knew she only had seconds left. Kate stuffed it underneath her jumper. It wasn't a thick file, but it was big enough to make an odd shape, and she crossed her arms over it, pushing the drawer shut with her foot. It clanged.

Julie's head whipped round to see Kate leaning against the cabinet. 'Everything all right?' asked Kate quickly.

Julie looked at her closely for a moment. 'Yes, they've nearly finished. I don't know if your friend will be getting what he wanted though. Mr Ballios didn't look pleased.'

As long as we can get out of here as fast as possible, thought Kate, horribly aware of the bulge in her jumper.

'Was there anything else?' asked Julie, her voice hardening slightly.

Oh no! She's seen I'm hiding something! Kate panicked. 'What age can you start ballet?' she blurted. 'It's just that my mum always loved the ballet . . .' *No she didn't!* 'And she died three years ago, and ever since then I've wondered if it was too late for me to start . . .' She let her mouth droop.

'Oh,' said Julie, instantly sympathetic. 'Oh, good-ness, you poor thing. You can start any age, love. I've got a friend who took it up in her thirties. Do you want me to give you the number of my girls' ballet school?'

Kate opened her eyes wide. 'Oh, would you?' *I can't believe I'm doing this!* For a moment she felt guilty for telling such lies to this nice woman. Not to mention using the fact that her mother had died to distract attention away from the file under her jumper.

Julie sat down again at her desk and picked up her mobile, scrolling through the numbers. 'Here you go, love.' She scribbled the number onto a jotter, tore off the page and held it out.

Kate somehow managed to take the note without uncrossing her arms. 'Thanks so much, that's really kind of you.'

'Any time, love, and I'm so sorry to hear about your mum.'

The office door opened, and Simon came out, looking somewhat red in the face. Behind him stood a dark man, with very broad shoulders emphasized by the style of his jacket. He was frowning. 'Next time, send your father,' he told Simon sharply.

Simon's face flushed redder.

Dimitri Ballios turned to Julie. 'I've got to get that

contract finished by six. I don't want to be disturbed again.'

The door slammed.

Julie looked as though she wasn't sure what to say.

'Come on,' said Simon to Kate. 'Let's get out of here.'

There was nothing Kate wanted more, especially as she felt like the file was burning a hole in her jumper, but she needed to make doubly sure that Julie wasn't suspicious. 'Are you all right?' she asked him, with a sideways flick of her eyes to the receptionist.

Simon instantly understood. His shoulders slumped. 'He won't even listen to me,' he said dejectedly. 'It's no use.'

'Oh,' said Kate. 'I'm really sorry.' She went to touch him on his arm, but remembered she was holding the file and hurriedly pulled her hand back. 'We'd better go then. It was worth a try.'

'Yeah, I guess so.'

Kate turned to Julie. 'Thanks for the ballet number,' she said. 'And I hope your girls have had a good lesson.'

Julie beamed, all previous suspicion forgotten. 'Thank you, love. And I hope your sister,' she said to Simon, 'finds some way to have her operation.'

Simon looked bewildered. 'Oh, thanks.'

'Come on,' said Kate, alarmed that just at the last minute they might be found out. 'Got to catch our bus.'

'Bye,' Julie called after them.

Kate and Simon didn't say anything at all until they were down the stairs and out on the street again. Then Simon turned to her. 'Well?' His eyes were alight with expectation.

Kate sighed. 'Sorry.'

His face fell. 'Oh. Oh well, never mind.'

Kate pulled out the file with a flourish. 'Just kidding! Look!'

Simon's jaw dropped. 'You never! Kate, that's awesome! What's in it?'

'Don't know yet.' She started to open the file, but a small piece of paper was caught by the breeze and went flying down the street. 'Catch it!'

Simon darted after it and rescued the tiny scrap. 'We'd better look at it inside. There's a library over there.'

Finding a spare table, the two of them sat down and spread the contents of the file out in front of them. 'There's not much,' said Kate, disappointed.

Simon was staring intently. 'This is a list of Tilworths opening times,' he said. 'And look – here's a list of names of people who work there, and what shifts they do.' He turned over the page and whistled. 'And on the back there's a list of security and fences and where there are padlocks.' He looked up at Kate. 'Why would he need this unless he was planning to break in?'

'It's not exactly evidence though, is it?' asked Kate. 'What else is there?' She reached for another sheet and her eyes widened. 'This is a list of all the break-ins and vandalism. Look – it's got the rock through the roof and the brick through the window and everything.'

'What's that written next to them?'

'Names.' Kate squinted. The writing was hard to read. 'Smithy, Craig, Andy. And there's a number too. Next to Smithy it says twenty. Twenty what?'

Simon bit his lip. 'I don't know. But do you think, since there's a name next to each one . . .'

'They're the ones who did it?' finished Kate. 'You mean, this Smithy person broke the window?'

'What else could it mean?'

'Twenty . . .' mused Kate. 'Twenty what? Twenty minutes? No – maybe he lives at number twenty?'

'Twenty pounds?' suggested Simon quietly.

'Twenty pounds? Why would it be . . . Oh!' Kate clapped a hand to her mouth. 'You mean, he was *paid* to break the window?'

'And Craig was paid ten pounds to throw a rock through the roof.' Simon gazed at the paper.

'So all the little things . . . Mr Ballios was behind the whole thing? He planned it all?' She swallowed. 'Do you think . . . this would be enough for the police?'

Simon was still holding the scrap of paper he'd rescued outside. He glanced down at it and his hand began to shake. 'I think this might help,' he said, and his voice wobbled with excitement. He held out the paper. 'It's a receipt. For eight tubs of caustic soda. And he paid with his own credit card!'

Chapter 13

Garden marigold

'There's one for me in three minutes,' Simon said, glancing up at the scrolling bus information display. 'What about you?'

'Two minutes.'

'Cool.' He hesitated. 'Do you think we did the right thing? I mean, do you think it will really get to DS Kemmitt?'

Kate stared up the road towards the police station. After waiting for half an hour to be seen, they had handed over the precious file to a bored-looking constable who had told them it would be passed on to the relevant authority. Having felt so excited that they had found such vital evidence, she now felt disappointed at the formality of the police station. 'I hope so. Maybe we can ring up tomorrow and remind them?'

Simon nodded. 'That's a good idea. Don't want

that file to end up in the bin by mistake!'

Kate laughed, but she was still anxious. What if someone thought the file didn't look important enough? What if they threw it away without realizing its significance? 'I'm sure as soon as anyone reads it, they'll see just how important it is,' she said hopefully. 'I mean, it's going to prove his guilt, isn't it?'

'Yeah . . .' Simon's voice was dejected. 'I guess it will.'

Kate glanced at him in sudden awareness. She had been talking about proving a man guilty of the attack, but it wasn't just any man, was it? Dimitri Ballios was Simon's uncle – his own *family*. She opened her mouth to ask him if he was sorry they'd gone to the police, but something stopped her. What if he said yes? What if Simon was already regretting their actions – what if he wished they'd never visited Dimitri in the first place?

Worse, what if he ended up blaming *her* for putting his uncle in prison?

They stood in silence for a few more moments. *It's no good*, decided Kate. *I have to ask him. It'd be better to know for sure if he's angry with me.* 'Simon, are you—' she began.

'Number seventy-three,' Simon interrupted, as a bus approached. 'That's yours, isn't it?'

'Yes, but—'

'And that's mine, right behind it.' He reached into his pocket. 'I guess we just have to wait and see what happens.'

Kate's bus pulled alongside the stop. Panic rose in her throat. Was he angry with her? She had to know! 'Simon, I just have to ask—'

'Are you getting on or not?' asked a man behind her impatiently.

'I'll see you tomorrow,' Simon said, starting for the second bus. 'You can ask me then.'

'Hurry up,' said the impatient man, and Kate hastily got onto her bus. As she found a seat, Simon's bus pulled out to overtake, and within seconds she had lost sight of it altogether. She rubbed her eyes. *Tomorrow*, she decided. *Tomorrow I'll make sure he's OK. Because I don't want him to blame me, if . . . if everything goes wrong for his family.*

♥

Her father opened the door as she approached. 'Where have you been? I was so worried about you!'

'Really?' Kate didn't intend her tone to be sharp but she was still worrying about Simon.

'*Kate*,' said Nick, an edge to his voice. 'Where were

you? Anpa told me you were going to be staying on at work for another hour, but it's nearly half past seven!'

'Sorry,' said Kate, without really meaning it. *He doesn't seem to care where I am most of the time, does he? He's always at work!* 'It took longer than I thought. Where's Anpa?'

'Gone to bed. Listen, Kate . . .'

'Why's he in bed? It's still early.'

Nick ran a hand through his hair. 'I don't know, he said he was tired. Kate, you *must* make sure you keep in touch. I tried your mobile but it was switched off.'

'Oh – yeah, sorry.' The news about Anpa had distracted her from the events of the afternoon. 'Is he all right? Is he ill?'

'No, he said he'd be fine. Oh, and Megan rang. She's back from holiday, she wants you to call her back.'

'OK.' Kate was hardly listening now. She put down her bag and keys and made for the stairs.

'Kate . . .'

'I'm going to see Anpa, OK?' She heard her father sigh in exasperation as she headed up to Anpa's room.

Anpa was lying in bed, his eyes closed, his breathing regular. Kate stood in the doorway. It wasn't like him at all to go to bed at this time of the evening. It wasn't even dark outside. She watched him for a few minutes, wondering if he would wake up and ask for some tea. Every now and then, something flickered across his face; a twitch of pain maybe? Or was he just dreaming?

There didn't seem to be anything for her to do, so she closed the door quietly and went into her father's room to borrow the telephone.

'Hi, Megan, it's me.'

'Kate!' Megan's voice seemed very loud suddenly, and Kate hurried into her own room to close the door. 'Hey, how are you? We're just back!'

'Yeah, Dad told me.'

'It was brilliant! But everything is a huge mess now, and Owen's refusing to go to bed because he slept on the plane and says he isn't tired at all.' Megan sounded amused. 'He keeps wanting to get out all these toys to play with. I swear Mum's going to smack him in a minute.' There was a rustle. 'Ooh! Wait till you see my tan! I'm not even going to need the fake stuff at the next dance competition!' A cacophony of voices. 'Hang on, Owen wants to talk to you.'

There was a scrabbling and then a very loud, 'HELLO, KATE.'

Kate held the handset away from her ear. 'Hi, Owen, how are you?'

'FINE.'

There was another pause and then Megan came back on the line. 'He never knows what to say on the phone, it's so funny. So how are things with you? How's the job going?'

Kate took a breath. How on earth could she explain? 'It's good. Only there was a bit of a break-in a few days ago. Someone destroyed the plants and we had to close for a bit. We're open again now though.'

'Oh my God, that sounds horrendous! Is everyone OK?'

'Yes, we're fine. Listen, Megan, I'll tell you all about it when I next see you.'

Megan instantly understood. 'Course. I know it's a bit mad here, it's not a good time to talk. I just wanted to say hi.'

Kate smiled. 'Thanks. I'm so glad you're back.'

'Me too. To tell you the truth . . .' Megan's voice turned into an intense whisper, 'the last few days have been kind of hard. I mean, I love my family and I love Jake and his family, but everyone has been getting on each other's nerves and I think we were all glad to leave.' She gave a snort. 'Jake's mum has driven us mad with her obsession with sun cream too. I'll tell you about it another time. You around tomorrow evening then?'

'Yes, that should be OK.'

'Great – can I come round? Or do you want to come round to mine?'

'I don't mind.'

'Come round here then. In fact, why don't you come round when you've finished work, and you can have tea here?'

'I'll need to check . . .'

'No problem. Let me know if you can't, otherwise I'll see you tomorrow.'

Kate sat for a few minutes on her bed and closed her eyes. For the first time today there was peace. It had been too busy, she thought, too much had happened in a short space of time. She wasn't entirely sure what to make of it, either. Had she really gone to Dimitri Ballios's office and stolen a file from under his receptionist's nose? Had she really lied to Anpa and her father about where she'd been? It didn't seem like the new Kate at all! It was far more like something the old Kate would have done. A daredevil, Tasha had called her – if Tasha could only see her now! Kate smiled and shook her head. There was no doubt, it *had* been kind of exciting . . . Maybe being quiet and calm and safe was just a little bit . . . *boring*, sometimes?

'Kate! Dinner's on the table!'

She sighed. She had to go down and face her father. The trouble was, talking to him these days took such an effort. She could barely remember the time he used to laugh easily, his eyes crinkling at the corners. She heaved herself off the bed.

'You OK?' Nick asked as she sat down at the table. His voice sounded uncertain, as though he wasn't sure of her reaction.

'Just tired,' she admitted.

'I found some salmon in the freezer,' he said. 'Hope it's all right.'

'It looks nice.' *We're tiptoeing around a conversation*, she thought wearily. *Again. But nothing's going to change, is it?* She felt a sudden flash of irritation. *And he should be making more of an effort. He's my father, isn't he? Why can't he act more like one?*

Nick saw her lips tighten, and he sighed.

This was going to be a long and silent meal.

Chapter 14

Mandrake

At first, Kate wasn't sure what had woken her up. She glanced at the clock. 3.16 a.m.

'Unnh.'

Kate's head felt fuzzy from sleep, but that had definitely been a moan. Briefly, panic flashed through her head. Was there someone in the house? Were they attacking Anpa or her dad? But the panic passed when she heard the moan again. It was her grandfather, she was sure of it. And he never made sounds like that.

Before she had even thought about getting up, Kate was on her feet and heading out of her room. She pushed open Anpa's door. He was curled up in bed, still groaning. 'Anpa? Are you all right?'

'Indigestion,' he grunted.

Kate switched on the bedside light and was shocked at his appearance. Her grandfather looked pale and sweaty, his face creased in pain. 'Indigestion? Are you sure?'

Anpa nodded, though another spasm gripped him and he grimaced in pain. 'Just ... need ... Gaviscon ...' he panted. 'In bathroom.'

Kate dashed to the bathroom and scrabbled around for the green bottle. Her father suddenly appeared in the doorway, yawning and rubbing his head. 'Kate? What are you doing in the bathroom? Are you all right?' But then he too heard Anpa's groans and his eyes widened.

The two of them hurried back to Anpa's side. He was panting, and his arms hugged his chest. 'He said it was indigestion,' said Kate, frightened, the bottle of Gaviscon in her hand.

'It looks worse than that to me,' replied Nick. He bent down to Anpa. 'John, can you hear me? Can you tell me where it hurts?'

'Chest,' gasped Anpa. 'Can't ... breathe ... sitting on ... my chest.'

Nick swung round to Kate. 'I think we need to call an ambulance.'

'What!'

'It could be serious, Kate. Get the phone.'

Kate was so anxious she dropped the phone as she fetched it from her father's room. She heard him snap, 'Hurry up!' and there was a note of fear in his voice.

'Ambulance,' Nick said abruptly into the phone. Then he paused. 'It's my father-in-law. He's got chest pains. I think he might be having a heart attack.' He listened for a moment and then turned to Kate. 'Go downstairs and unlock the front door. Put the outside light on, so the paramedics can come straight in.'

Kate stumbled down the stairs, her breath rattling in her throat. Heart attack? No, no, surely not! Anpa couldn't die! *Not him too!* Her fingers shook as she unlocked the door and flicked the light switch.

When she reached the top of the stairs, she heard her father say into the phone, 'Wouldn't paracetamol do? I don't know if we've got any aspirin. Oh. Oh, I see. Hang on.'

Kate called, 'I'll get it!' and ducked into the bathroom again, sweeping the contents of the cabinet onto the floor. Paracetamol . . . ibuprofen . . . aspirin! 'I've got some!' she yelled, and took it through to Nick. 'I'll get some water.'

'No!' he called back. 'No water – he has to chew it.'

Kate didn't have time to feel puzzled. Nick popped a tablet out of the packet and forced it into Anpa's mouth. Anpa was lying back now, his face getting paler by the minute, and his breathing rasping in his chest. 'Chew it,' ordered Nick.

'Where's the ambulance?' asked Kate in a tight voice. 'We need it now!'

'It's coming,' Nick told her, and then listened to the voice on the end of the phone again. 'I can try,' he said, before putting the handset on the bed. 'Kate, give me a hand. We have to get John's legs raised up.'

The two of them struggled with pillows and an unresponsive Anpa. 'Can't we do something else?' Kate cried. 'To help him?'

'He needs proper help,' Nick said, wrestling to stuff a couple of pillows under Anpa's legs. 'Defibrillators, things like that. And oxygen.'

'There must be *something* we can do!'

At that moment, Anpa leaned over the side of the bed and was sick. Kate jumped back in shock. Anpa had never had a day ill as long as she could remember. 'They're on their way,' Nick said, seeing her face. He picked up the phone. 'All right, we've done that. He's just been sick.'

'I should clear it up,' said Kate, desperate for something to do.

'Leave it!' snapped Nick. Then he listened to the phone. 'Go downstairs,' he said to Kate suddenly. 'The ambulance is nearly here.'

Kate missed the bottom step of the stairs, jarring her ankle as she landed awkwardly. She could already see the flashing lights as she wrenched open the front door. The ambulance pulled up and a man and a woman jumped out, each carrying a large case. 'Hello, love,' said the woman. 'Where should we go?'

'Upstairs. He's upstairs. Oh, please.'

They ran up the stairs and straight into Anpa's room, and then everything became a blur for Kate. She could see just past her father to the bed, where the paramedics were a haze of green, moving rapidly from checking Anpa's pulse and eyes to strapping an oxygen mask on his face and listening to his heart. Within minutes they had got him down the stairs and into the back of the ambulance, and Kate hadn't even heard them tell Nick where they were taking him.

'Do you want to come with him?' the woman asked Nick.

He hesitated and looked back at Kate. 'I want to come too,' she said.

'We'll follow in the car,' Nick told the paramedic, who nodded briskly and jumped into the ambulance. Seconds later, it pulled away from the kerb, blue lights flashing silently in the darkness.

'Get dressed,' Nick told Kate, but she was already running up the stairs to her room to find her clothes.

The hospital wasn't far, but every minute felt like an hour to Kate. There was hardly anyone else on the roads at this time, which was just as well because Nick's face was set with concentration and he barely glanced around at junctions. Kate knew how he felt: she had an uncontrollable urge to get to the hospital. Anpa shouldn't be on his own; if the two of them were there, he might pull through this, but what if he died and they weren't there?

Mum died when I wasn't there . . .

Kate and Nick tore through the car park to the main doors of Accident and Emergency, and gasped out their names to the receptionist, who nodded and told them to take a seat.

Kate suddenly felt like collapsing. It was like running as fast as possible straight into a brick wall. She was stunned. 'We need to see him,' she said urgently to the receptionist, who smiled sympathetically and told her Anpa was in the best hands possible and it was best if she stayed out here. 'You can't do anything to help right now,' she said kindly. 'I'll get someone to come and talk to you as soon as they can.'

Kate's knees weakened, and she was secretly glad when Nick led her to a chair. 'Where is he?' she whispered.

He shrugged helplessly. 'I don't know, Kate. Having

tests done maybe? He might even be in surgery. The receptionist is right; we'd only get in the way.'

'But he's surrounded by strangers.'

'He's ill,' Nick said, reaching for her hand and squeezing it. 'He'll know he's being looked after, that's the main thing.'

Kate shook her head. It wasn't right, Anpa having to go through all of this without a friendly face. She looked around at the large open waiting space and shivered. Kate hated hospitals. Hospital was where her mother had spent so many hours and days towards the end of her life, having chemicals pumped into her and radio waves shot at her. Which didn't work anyway. Kate had wanted to come to her mother's treatments but Cynthia insisted she stay away. So instead she had got used to her cheerful mother leaving in the morning to be returned later in the day weak, grey and sick. And sometimes to be kept in overnight whilst new scans and investigations took place. Kate hated hospital because it had taken her mother away from her. And it had sent Kate and her father home 'for some rest' while her mother slipped away from life, alone in her room.

Time passed slowly. When the initial adrenalin rush had worn off, Kate and Nick simply sat and stared at the walls. 'Should have thought to pick up a book,' commented Nick at one point, but Kate knew she wouldn't be able to read. Thoughts chased each other around the walls of her mind; memories of her mother, images of Anpa bent double with pain, being sick, being carried down the stairs . . . She wished they hadn't had to come here, of all places. She'd always been told that hospital was where they made people better, but she knew that wasn't true any more. More than anything at that moment, she wished they hadn't called an ambulance. Maybe Anpa could have been treated at home, surrounded by his family?

The two of them sat side by side, each in their own little world. Kate felt so alone. *Anpa is my best friend*, she realized. *He's the only one who's been there for me over the past three years. Every time I needed someone, he was there. I couldn't bear it if . . .*

It was ninety minutes before someone came to talk to them, and by then Nick had been up to the front desk five times to ask if there was any news. The receptionist was starting to get annoyed.

'Are you the family of John Lumsden?' asked the young man dressed in hospital scrubs.

Nick immediately stood up. 'Yes. Is he – how is he?'

'Would you like to come through here?' asked the young man. 'It's easier to talk in a private room.'

Nick reached for his daughter's hand as they walked the few metres to the little interview room. His hand was cold and dry and it gave Kate little comfort. Had Anpa died? Surely the man would have said if he was still alive? Why did he want to talk to them in a private room? Was there bad news?

'Take a seat,' said the young man, and Nick and Kate sat obediently.

'My name is Rupesh Singh, and I'm an SHO here.'

A what? wondered Kate.

'Your father has had quite a serious cardiac arrest,' went on Mr Singh.

Nick interrupted, 'Father-in-law.'

'Oh, right. Sorry. He's come out of surgery and he's doing well.'

'What kind of surgery?' asked Nick.

'Angioplasty.'

'What's that?'

Mr Singh seemed taken aback to be asked for a description, but he did his best to patiently explain how a small balloon had been inserted into an artery and inflated so as to clear the blockage. 'He's being monitored closely in the Coronary Care Unit,' he told them, 'just to make sure there aren't any complications.' He finally gave them a smile. 'But he's come through the first two hours, which is a very good sign.'

'Can we go and see him?' asked Kate in a small voice.

Mr Singh shook his head. 'Not for another hour or so, I'm afraid. We prefer visitors to wait until seven a.m. as there are other patients recuperating in the same bay and we like to keep it quiet overnight. And Mr Lumsden is very tired, of course.'

It's only five thirty! thought Kate. *I can't wait another hour and a half!* She squeezed her father's hand urgently.

Nick understood. 'Can't we pop in now? We'll be very quiet.'

Mr Singh was sympathetic. 'Sorry. You mustn't worry though, the signs are all very good. There's a large waiting area on the first floor; it's more comfortable than waiting in A and E.'

Nick put an arm round Kate's shoulders. 'That sounds like a good idea,' he said. 'Thanks for letting us know.'

Mr Singh nodded. 'I realize you've been waiting a while. It's not long now, and if there's any change or problem, we'll come and find you.'

♥

Kate and her father made their way to the waiting room on the first floor. It was quieter than downstairs, and the chairs were more comfortable. 'You should try to close your eyes,' Nick told her, but Kate was adamant.

'I can't, not while Anpa . . .' She trailed off.

'I know.'

They sat in silence, tired eyes watching the seconds tick by on the clock on the far wall.

'Kate . . .'

She jumped slightly.

'Sorry, I didn't realize you were nodding off.'

'I wasn't.'

He looked at her. 'Are you holding up OK?'

'I'm fine.'

Her father reached for her hand again. 'I'm sorry we're here. I know you must hate it. I do too.'

Kate didn't know what to say, so she said nothing.

'Just being here – the sounds, the smell . . . it brings it all back.' Nick was speaking very quietly. 'But, Kate, it's not the same.'

Kate made a small noise.

'No, it isn't. This is Anpa. He's had a heart attack. It's nothing like – the other thing.'

Suddenly she felt cross. '*The other thing?* You mean Mum, don't you? Why can't you just say so?'

He shrugged helplessly. 'I don't know. Maybe because I find it just as hard as you do to talk about it.'

'I only find it hard because you won't talk back,' she muttered, but he heard.

'I didn't want to upset you. I thought we'd all find it easier if we *didn't* talk about it. About – her.'

'Yeah, well, it isn't.' She pulled her hand away. 'It's like you're pretending she never existed.'

He stared at her in horror. 'What? I don't . . . that's not . . .' He lapsed into silence.

Kate knew she'd hurt him but she didn't feel sorry. He'd become so remote! She was *glad* he was having to think about it now! She sat and stared ahead with burning eyes.

Her dad let out a huge sigh. 'You want to get some breakfast?'

'I'm not hungry. I feel sick.'

'That's because you need something to eat.'

'I can't.'

'Some tea, then.' Nick stood up. 'I'll get us some from the machine down the hall. Extra sugar.'

Kate wrinkled her nose. She hated sugar in her tea.

No sooner had Nick walked away than the same Mr Singh came into the waiting area, his eyes finding her quickly in the expanse of empty chairs. Kate sat up, suddenly alert. 'Is my granddad all right?'

'Where's your father?' he asked.

'Gone to get some tea. How's Anpa?'

He sat down next to her. 'He's doing fine. I just came from there, and I know it's not quite time yet but the nurse in charge said it would be OK for you to go in a little early.'

Kate sprang to her feet. 'How do I get there?'

'Just follow the signs to CCU – Coronary Care Unit,' he told her. 'But wait for your dad.'

'Thanks,' she said over her shoulder, already hurrying after Nick. Where had he gone? There were three corridors! Where was the drinks machine? Kate swung desperately around. They needed to go! What if she went down one of the corridors and it turned out to be the wrong one, and Nick came up another one, holding the tea and they missed each other? Every moment she stood here was a second wasted!

How typically annoying of her father to choose this particular moment to go and find tea! Kate wished she could split herself into three, so that she could run down all the corridors at the same time. But just as she was coming to a decision to race down the one on her left, Nick rounded the corner to her right, carrying two steaming Styrofoam cups. 'They said we can go up early,' Kate told him, the words bursting out of her so loudly that the three other people in the corridor looked at her in surprise and disapproval.

'What, now?' said Nick, his face registering dismay. 'I just got the tea.'

'We haven't got time to drink it.'

'Can't you just hang on a minute?' Nick pleaded. 'I'll blow on it.'

'No! We have to go *now*!'

Her dad looked at her. He put the cups down on the top of a nearby bin. 'All right. Come on.'

The lift didn't come quickly enough for Kate. 'We should go up the stairs,' she suggested.

Her father looked at her sympathetically. 'Kate, nothing's going to happen to him in the next three minutes.'

'I know.' She couldn't explain. It was the thought that he was up there, on the ward, all alone. *Mum died when I wasn't there. She was all alone. If I can be with Anpa, then maybe he won't die . . .*

The lift finally arrived, and it took seconds to reach the right floor. Kate dashed out as soon as the doors opened, her eyes desperately seeking the blue CCU sign. 'This way!' Her father kept up as best he could. Through the double doors marked CORONARY CARE UNIT there was a reception desk, and Kate was soon panting out Anpa's name.

The lady behind the desk smiled kindly at her. 'Take a moment to catch your breath,' she said. 'I know who

you've come to see, but you can't see him in that state.
He needs peace and quiet, you understand?'

Kate gulped and nodded. Within a few moments,
her breathing had steadied, and the receptionist came
out from behind the desk to show them the way.

Kate felt sick as they rounded the corner of the
recovery bay. Memories of visiting her mother flooded
back, and she clutched the wall for support. Nick
grabbed her arm. 'You OK?'

'I'm fine.' Her eyes darted from one bed to another.
Where was he?

'Over by the window,' said her father quietly.

The receptionist said, 'You mustn't stay too long.
He's very tired. But I'm sure he'll be glad to see you.'

Anpa lay back on the white pillows, his familiar
wrinkled face turned towards the brightening sky. It
was hard to believe that only a few hours earlier he
had been doubled over in pain. A tube ran out of his
arm up to a drip, and a machine sat silently flashing
next to the bed. 'Anpa?' whispered Kate.

'He's asleep. Don't wake him.'

But Anpa turned his head. It took a moment or
two for his eyes to focus, then he smiled at Kate.
'Hello.'

Quite suddenly and without any warning, Kate
burst into choking sobs.

Anpa's forehead creased in concern. 'Don't cry,' he said in a low voice, but he made no attempt to sit up. Instead he lifted his hand a little way off the bed. 'Come and sit with me.'

Nick pulled up a chair and Kate sat, her eyes and nose streaming. 'I'll get some tissues,' he murmured, and disappeared.

Kate wiped her nose on her sleeve and tried to control her sobs, which sounded so loud in the peaceful ward. 'Sorry, Anpa.' Her voice wouldn't behave itself – it wobbled all over the place. And no matter how hard she tried, tears kept flowing down her cheeks.

Anpa patted her hand. 'It's all right.' His voice was very quiet – so quiet Kate could only just hear it – and every movement looked like an effort. 'I'm doing OK. They say . . .' his eyes closed briefly, 'they say I'll be home in a few days.'

'I'm so glad you're all right.' Kate squeezed his hand as gently as she could. 'I thought . . . I thought . . .'

'But it didn't happen,' said Anpa, reading her mind. 'They fixed me.' His eyes closed. 'Sorry. Very . . . tired . . .'

Kate sat quietly until her father came back, clutching a handful of toilet roll. 'Sorry, all I could find.'

His face was pale, his eyes shiny, and his voice trembled. 'Has he gone to sleep?'

'I think so. Thanks.' Kate blew her nose and wiped her eyes. 'He said he was doing OK. The doctors told him he'll be home in a few days.'

'There you go. We should probably let him rest.'

'I want to stay here.'

Her father looked around for another chair but couldn't see one. He leaned on the end of the bed. 'Kate, you look shocking. You need some sleep – we both do. He's got to rest anyway. And that lady said we shouldn't stay long.'

'I'm not going.' Kate felt the tears rise again. 'What if he dies and we're not here?' she whispered. 'Like Mum? I can't leave him.'

Nick stared at her for a moment. 'Oh Kate, is that what you've been thinking? Kate, love . . .' He came over to stand next to her and put a hand on her shoulder. 'He's not going to die,' he said quietly. 'He's come through the surgery, hasn't he? That Mr Singh said the first couple of hours were the most important. And you know how strong he is. Your Anpa's a fighter.'

'Mum was a fighter too . . .'

'That's true.' He was silent for a moment. 'But she had a long battle, Kate. And the enemy was stronger in the end. It didn't help that she was so weak from all the treatment.'

'She was alone.'

'No she wasn't. We'd all been there that day – you, me, Anpa. She knew we loved her. And we all knew the end could come any time.'

'*I* didn't.'

'Yes, you did, love.' He reached to tilt her chin up to him. 'She told you. You just didn't believe it.'

'But we should have been there when she . . . when she . . .' Tears spilled again.

Nick pulled her up into a hug. 'I know how you feel,' he said in a whisper. 'I've wished the same thing for the past three years. But it won't change what happened, Kate.'

'You never said . . .'

'Why talk about something you can't change?'

Kate pushed him away, wiping her eyes angrily. 'You don't want to talk to me anyway,' she said. 'You never want to talk to me these days. You never come home, you never want to spend time with me.'

'That's not true . . .' But he wouldn't meet her eye.

'And I know why.' Kate fixed him with a fierce glare. 'It's because I'm nothing like her, isn't it? It's because whereas she was all bright and clever and pretty, I'm just – just ordinary and stupid . . . and . . .'

'*What?*'

Anpa made a mumbling noise in his sleep. Nick glanced at him and reached out to pull Kate away from the bed and into the corridor. 'Don't ever, *ever* say that! You're not ordinary, *or* stupid! You're the most precious thing . . . You have *no* idea . . .' He shook his head helplessly. 'It's nothing to do with you. I love you just as much as I ever did.'

'But . . .' Kate felt even more confused. 'But then why don't you want to spend time with me any more?'

'I do, it's just that work—'

'Oh, you *always* say it's work!'

'It is . . .' Nick started to say, and then he looked down. 'You're right. That's just an excuse. I don't know, Kate, how can I explain? When your mum died, I thought the light had gone out of my life.'

That's how I felt too.

'Anything I saw that reminded me of her just – hurt. It made me ache, seeing her jewellery, her clothes, photos of her flower displays, even scraps of paper with her writing on. I thought I could make it easier by hiding all her things away, but that house . . . we bought it together, it's the only house we ever lived in as a couple. Every *room* in that house has memories. I walk up the stairs, I remember her laugh. I go into your bedroom, I see her sitting there smiling, telling me I'm going to be a dad.' His voice cracked. 'And I need to keep busy. I have to keep *thinking*, because if I don't, if I relax – I think of *her*. Work helps – it stops me thinking about other things. It fills up my brain so there's no room for sadness or grief.' He sighed. 'That's why I haven't even been able to consider a holiday. All that *time* and nothing to do but *remember* . . .'

Kate felt numb. 'You don't – hate me?' she whispered.

'Hate *you*?' In three steps he was holding her tight. 'Of course not,' he said softly in her ear. 'How could I hate someone so important to me?'

Chapter 15

White Clover

'I've called Tilworths to say you won't be in,' Nick said, as they sat down with their breakfast trays in the canteen. 'Janet says they all send their love.'

Kate nodded. Tilworths, Simon, Dimitri Ballios . . . it all seemed like a far-off dream today. She found it hard to believe that only a few hours ago, she and Simon had delivered the stolen file to the police station. She wondered vaguely whether Simon had called DS Kemmitt, but she wasn't sure she cared right now. Having felt sick at the very idea of eating, she was now finding that the smell of sausage and egg was making her tummy rumble loudly.

'I tried to ring John's brother,' Nick said through a mouthful of toast. 'The one who lives in Scotland, who you've never met. I left a message, but I don't suppose he'd want to come all this way to visit. He must be nearly ninety by now.'

For a moment, Kate felt sad that Anpa didn't have a bigger family; more people to care about him. *But he has us*, she reminded herself. *We care enough for twenty relatives*.

They spent the day at the hospital, sometimes sitting on benches outside when the visiting hours closed. Anpa was very tired and dozed for most of the time, but Nick and Kate kept themselves amused by reading celebrity magazines from the waiting area and playing cards with a battered pack lent by a patient in one of the other beds in Anpa's bay.

At half past five in the evening, Anpa sat up in bed and said he'd like a packet of humbugs. Nick and Kate looked at each other and grinned, and Nick immediately picked up his jacket and said he'd go and find some. 'Is he allowed them?' Kate whispered so that Anpa couldn't hear her.

Nick shrugged. 'Can't see how humbugs will do any harm. But I might get soft mints instead so he doesn't choke on them.'

'OK. Where will you get them?'

'I'll see if the shop downstairs does sweets. You know, the one that sells balloons and cards. If not, I'll nip across the road to the newsagent's.' He glanced at the clock. 'We have to leave in half an hour anyway, visiting hours will be over. Just keep him entertained.'

216

'Now,' said Anpa, when Nick had gone, 'we can talk properly.'

Kate smiled. This was the Anpa she knew! 'Talk about what?'

'You.'

'Me?'

Anpa took her hand and settled himself more comfortably on his pillows. 'I've been thinking,' he said, 'about your future.'

Kate was startled. 'What do you mean?'

'You're a good girl, Kate. You're kind and you work hard. That language-of-flowers idea you came up with for Tilworths – it's fantastic. Your mother would have loved it. And I think you've got real creativity when it comes to flowers. You should think about floristry as a future career.'

'I could never be as good as Mum.'

'You mustn't put yourself down so much. You've got more brains than you think. Which is why . . .' he leaned forward, 'I want to put some money aside for you. For the future.'

'You don't have to do that.'

'I want to.' He nodded vigorously. 'You've got the money your mum left you, of course, but that's for buying a car or a deposit for a house, or something in a few years. This is different. Maybe some time you might want to go to college or take an apprenticeship. Maybe one day you might even want to run your own business. You'll need some money to get you started.'

'But Anpa, you'll still be around to help me.'

He smiled. 'No, I won't. Not for ever. This whole heart-attack thing – it's made me realize something. When I go, I go. It'll be all right.'

'Don't talk like that.'

'Listen.' He put his hand on hers and pressed firmly. 'You've got to understand. I'm ready. When it comes. I've had a great life – and the best part has been watching you grow up.' His expression softened. 'You're a lovely girl, Kate. You're kind and thoughtful and you've got a lot going for you. But you've buried that spark you used to have, and it's time to move on. You can't hide away for the rest of your life. Let down some of those barriers. Seize the moment.'

Kate blinked away sudden tears at the kindness in his voice. 'I am trying, Anpa,' she said quietly.

'I know you are, love. Working at Tilworths has really brought you out of your shell, but it's nearly time to go back to school. I don't want to see you slip back into the girl who won't say boo to a goose. That won't get you anywhere in life.' He squeezed her hand again. 'I know you've had a very hard few years. No one should go through what you've been through.

But don't deny yourself the chance of happiness, of a strong future, because of something bad that happened to you.'

Kate felt a tear slide down her cheek. 'I'll try,' she whispered.

'Good girl.' Anpa grinned suddenly. 'And I'm going to put some money away for when you decide to exhibit your flower arrangements at Chelsea!'

♥

When Nick came back with the soft mints, he found Kate and Anpa laughing together. 'What's the joke?' he asked.

'We're planning Kate's future for her,' Anpa told him, a broad smile on his face, though his eyes looked tired.

Nick looked at his daughter, her wild brown curls framing her freckled face. 'Something exciting, I hope,' he suggested, smiling at her.

Kate hesitated for a moment. 'Anpa wants me to become a florist.'

Her father put down the sweets. 'What an excellent idea.' He swallowed. 'Your mother would be very proud.'

Kate and Anpa glanced at each other. It was so

rarely that Nick mentioned Cynthia.

Nick saw the look, and took a breath. 'I've decided to sell the house,' he said firmly.

Anpa's mouth fell open. 'Sell the house? Why?'

'I'm sorry, John,' Nick said. 'I know you like it, but it's just got too many memories. Kate and I had a bit of a talk this morning . . . well, anyway, she made me see a few things. One of the reasons I work such long hours is so I don't have to come back to that house – the one where Cynthia and I were so happy.'

Anpa nodded slowly. 'I get it.'

'Don't worry,' Nick said, 'I'm sure we'll find something just as nice. And you'll come with us, of course.'

Kate's phone beeped suddenly. 'It's a text from Megan. Oh, I completely forgot I was supposed to be going round to hers! She wants to know where I am!'

'You should go home and get some rest,' Anpa told them. 'Quite enough excitement for one day.'

'I agree.' Nick turned to his daughter. 'Tell Megan you won't be able to make it this evening. We'll come back tomorrow, all right?'

'You're both to go into work tomorrow,' Anpa said firmly. 'Come and see me at the end of the day. I'll be fine. Besides, I'll be home soon. And while I'm having to sit around all day, I can plan the garden for next year!'

♥

Kate rang Megan on the way home. 'Sorry,' she said. 'I was at the hospital.'

Megan listened to Kate's explanation and immediately said, 'Of course, I completely understand. Send me a text when you're free.'

'I will.' Kate yawned. 'Sorry, I'm just really tired.'

'Talk to you soon. Send Anpa my love when you see him.'

'You should take the morning off work tomorrow,' Nick said as he drove carefully through the streets of Parchester.

Kate opened her mouth to say, 'I can't,' but her phone beeped again.

Hi its Simon hope evrythng OK

'Are you all right?' asked Nick. 'You look a bit funny.'

'I'm fine.' But Kate knew she was blushing. How had Simon got her number? 'It's just a text from Simon – you know, from work.'

'Really?' Her father shot her a sideways look. 'Do you *like* this boy, Kate?'

'Of course not . . .' Kate started to say, but she stopped. *Why not admit it, after all?* She looked down at her phone again. 'Maybe a bit.'

He sighed. 'I suppose it had to come eventually. You're growing up.' He looked rueful. 'I seem to have missed a lot of you growing up the past three years. I'm sorry, love. Things will be different now, I promise.'

'Yeah. I know.' And somewhere, deep inside, she knew they would. It was a good feeling.

♥

'Hi.'

'It's me, Kate.' It had taken her ten minutes to get up the courage to call him, and now he'd actually answered the phone, she wished she'd sent a text instead.

'Yes, I know, your name came up. I, um . . . how are you?'

'I'm all right.'

'Janet said your grandpa was ill.'

'Yes, he had a heart attack last night.' *Was it only last night? It feels like more than a day has passed.*

'Oh, wow, I'm so sorry. Is he . . .' He hesitated.

'He's in hospital,' Kate replied. 'He's going to be OK, they think.'

'That's great.' Simon sounded relieved.

There was a pause.

'Is everything OK at the centre?' asked Kate finally.

'Yeah, yeah, it's fine.'

'Have you heard anything from the police about that file?'

'No, not yet. I tried ringing DS Kemmitt this morning but someone just took a message and said she'd ring back, but she hasn't.'

'Oh.'

There was another pause. *This is so hard!* thought Kate. Talking to Simon had become quite easy; comfortable even the last couple of weeks – but talking on the phone was another matter! 'So . . .' she said, without any idea of what to say next.

'Yeah.'

She knew she should suggest hanging up – they'd said all they needed to say. But there was a cosy warm feeling in her stomach that he'd thought to contact her in the first place. He wanted to make sure she was all right – and just hearing his voice made her feel kind of queasy, in a good way. 'How did you get my number?' she asked, thankful she'd thought of something to talk about.

'Oh . . .' Simon sounded slightly embarrassed. 'I looked it up. In the staff room there's a book with everyone's details in it.'

Kate was glad he couldn't see her blushing. He cared enough to look it up himself!

'Don't tell Janet – I don't think she likes people going through the personal files, though it's up on the shelf for anyone to see.'

'I won't tell.' After the crazy events of the last twenty-four hours, talking to Simon made her feel calmer again. *Calm – and nervous at the same time*, she admitted to herself.

'Yeah. Well . . . guess I should go,' said Simon.

Kate wanted to say, *No, don't go, keep talking to me!* but it would sound silly, wouldn't it? So instead she said, 'OK, I'll see you tomorrow.'

'You're coming in?' Simon was surprised.

'Yeah.'

'Cool.' It was just one word, but the way he said it made Kate blush again. 'See you then.'

'Bye.'

'Bye.'

Kate stared at her phone for a moment, her finger hesitating over the 'disconnect' button. She felt a strange reluctance to press it. *You're being ridiculous!* she said to herself – but the phone remained connected to Simon's. *He* hadn't pressed the button either . . .

'Kate? You still there?'

Hastily, she held the phone to her ear again. 'Yes – yes, I'm here.'

'I just wanted to say – uh . . .' He paused.

Kate waited for what seemed like an age. 'Yes?'

'It'll be good to see you tomorrow. Bye.' The phone went dead.

Kate smiled and hugged herself. It would be good to see him too.

Chapter 16

Lily of the valley

'It's lovely to see you,' Janet told Kate the next morning. 'What a terrible shock you've all had.'

Kate nodded, her eyes flicking across to where Simon was sitting cross-legged on the shop floor, pricing up some new stock before the centre opened its doors. He looked up at her and smiled, and something in the region of her tummy button gave a wriggle. It was *very* nice to see him again. And Libby had been right – he was really very good-looking . . .

'You didn't have to come in today, you know,' Janet said. 'We can manage. You look like you could do with more rest.'

Kate shook her head. 'Anpa told me to come in.'

'I see.' Janet smiled. 'Still ordering people around, is he?'

Kate couldn't help but smile back at that. 'He says he's feeling a lot better.'

'He must be. Come along with me. I've got something to show you.'

'This is looking so different!' commented Kate with surprise. The whole outside area was now open to the public, and half the shelves were filled with plants, hastily brought through from the nursery. 'I can't believe you got all this done yesterday.'

'Mike and I stayed up most of the night working,' Janet replied. Her expression clouded. 'Though I'm not sure it's worth it any more, not if we're going to be targeted again.' She led the way along the passage to the nursery. 'There you are.'

Kate blinked in surprise. The bench in front of her was laden with flowering plants – roses, lilies, carnations, daisies . . . 'Where did all these come from?'

Janet smiled at her. 'Your display was selling so well, we wanted to make sure that it continued. We didn't have any plants ready here, so we bought these in from another garden centre.'

'You bought them?' Kate was astonished. 'But – how . . . ?'

'Don't worry, we got an excellent discount,' Janet said, pleased at Kate's reaction. 'In fact, don't tell anyone, but we only paid about twenty per cent of retail price. I have a friend at Parchester West, and they're all so sorry for what happened here. They even gave us fifteen ceramic pots for free.'

'Wow. That's – that's brilliant.'

'I'm hoping you can get the display up and running again by the end of the day.' Janet looked hopeful. 'Do you think that's possible?'

'Of course,' Kate said confidently.

'I know Simon does all the writing on the labels,' said Janet, 'so I'll send him over and you can tell him which ones to do.' She reached out to squeeze Kate's shoulder. 'I'm so glad your granddad is going to be all right. He's a great character.'

'Yeah, he is – thanks.'

Kate's stomach flipped as Simon appeared in the greenhouse doorway, and she hoped she wasn't blushing. 'Hi,' she said.

'Hi.' He gave her a big smile. 'You OK?'

'Yes. It's good to be back. It gives me something to do.'

'You still worried about your Anpa?'

It felt strange to hear him use her pet name. She shrugged. 'Sort of. I know I shouldn't be, but . . .' She hesitated. 'Well, you know my mum died. It was in hospital, and I wasn't there, and I always thought . . .'

Simon instantly understood. 'You don't want to leave him in case something bad happens.'

'Yes! That's exactly it!'

He looked sympathetic. 'It wouldn't make any difference though, would it? I mean, if you'd been there when your mum . . . wouldn't it have been worse, in a way? You'd have seen her – you know – die.'

Kate stared at him. *I hadn't thought of it like that.* 'But she might not have died, if I'd been there.'

Simon said slowly, 'I'm not saying you're wrong, but are you sure about that? People who are really ill . . . it's not like you being there would have stopped the illness. And your last memory of her would be, um . . . seeing her dead.' He screwed up his eyes at the word. 'Can't imagine that would be a good thing.'

'No . . .' Kate frowned. It was as though Simon's words had opened up an entirely new angle. 'I suppose not . . . at least this way I remember her alive.' She looked at him. 'Thank you. I hadn't ever thought of it that way.'

He smiled. 'Any time. You got a list for me? Janet said you were going to start work on the new display.'

'Oh – no, I haven't done a list yet. But I know them off by heart.'

He held out a sheet of paper and a pen. 'Here you go. Write them on that.'

Carefully, glancing at the plants every now and then, Kate wrote:

CARNATION – *Pure Love*
MICHAELMAS DAISY – *Innocence (New Baby)*
LILY – *Beauty*
RED ROSE – *I Love You*

Her hand shook slightly as she wrote the last one, and she felt herself blushing. *Good grief, what are you embarrassed about? That's what the flower means!* She handed the list to Simon. 'If you can do six of each, that'll be enough to start with.'

He squinted at it. 'Your handwriting is still really hard to read,' he commented. 'What does that last one say?'

Oh no! Kate swallowed. *Don't make me say it out loud!* 'Red rose.'

'Yes, but what does it say next to that? The pen's gone all blotchy.'

'Surely you can guess,' said Kate, trying to make a joke of it. 'It's a red rose, it only means one thing.'

'It looks like *I Awe You*.'

'I *love* you,' snapped Kate. *Oh God, I can't believe I just said it! And now I'm bright red!* She turned away quickly.

Simon cleared his throat. 'Right – sorry. Yeah, I see that now. I'll just – er . . .' He vanished.

Kate stood for a full minute, staring at the roses.

♥

'You have to tell him,' Megan said two days later, painting her toenails a vivid shade of purple. 'Before it's too late. I mean, you might not get another chance.'

Kate, sitting on Megan's bed, squirmed. 'I don't know how.'

'You just have to come out with it. Try not to think about it too much.'

'But what if he says no? Or worse?'

'Worse? What's worse?'

Kate bit her fingernail. 'What if he stops talking to me because he's so weirded out?'

Megan turned to look at her. 'Kate, that's hardly going to happen, is it? He might be a bit embarrassed. But if he is, so what? Another week and we'll be back at school. You'll never see him again.'

'I know . . .' Kate looked down at Megan's rug. It was pink with little hearts and flowers all over it.

'Well, think about it.' Megan pressed home her point. '*You'll never see him again* unless you say something!'

'But if he likes me, why hasn't *he* said something?'

'Maybe he's shy too.'

Kate sighed.

Megan giggled. 'You two are impossible. I want to lock you in a room or something and not let you out until you've agreed to go on a date.'

There was a knock at the door, and Megan's father stuck his head in. 'Just to let you know Owen and Mum are due back from swimming in about ten minutes, and I'm cooking dinner. Kate, are you staying?'

She shook her head regretfully. 'No, I have to go home, but thank you. Dad said he'd pick me up on his way back from the garage. He shouldn't be long now.'

'How's your grandfather?' asked Megan's dad.

'He's doing fine. You'd never know there'd been anything wrong!'

'He's home, then?'

'Not yet. But he says he's coming home tomorrow whether he's allowed or not. He's bored in the hospital. Keeps making trouble!'

Megan's dad grinned. 'Good for him. I'll give you a shout when your dad gets here, Kate.'

'Thanks.'

Megan screwed the top onto her nail varnish. 'So, back to Simon,' she said. 'Are you going to ask him out?'

'Oh, I don't know. Yes – no.' Kate just couldn't imagine herself doing such a thing. How on earth would she ever get the words out without making a complete idiot of herself?

'Well,' said Megan, admiring her toes, 'we're coming to Tilworths next week sometime for a new hose. If you haven't asked Simon out by then, I might have to do it for you!'

Kate's jaw dropped in horror. 'Don't you dare!'

Megan grinned at her. 'Then you'd better get on and do it yourself, hadn't you? Because you two are meant to be together, I just know it. And now that you're – I don't know – different . . .'

'What do you mean, different?'

Megan shook her head. 'It's hard to explain. You seem less – serious. You laugh more. I dunno, you just seem happier.'

Happier? Am I happier? Kate wondered. 'I suppose I am a bit,' she said slowly. 'It's been nice, working at Tilworths. I feel like I have a place; people listen to my ideas. It's sort of safe.'

Megan was nodding. 'I can tell.' She looked down at her toes again for a moment. 'Do you – think about your mum as much?'

'Maybe not as much as I did,' admitted Kate. 'Do you think that's bad?'

'No, not at all!' exclaimed Megan. 'I think it's *good* that you don't think about her all the time. I mean, obviously you're always going to miss her. But you've got your own life to lead, right?'

That's what Anpa said.

'And I'm sure she'd be proud of what you were doing – that display idea and all that,' added Megan. 'Wouldn't she?'

♥

On the way home, in the car, Kate wondered about it. She had thought that the best thing to do was to stay quiet, hidden, sad . . . better not to face the world because the world wasn't a happy place any more. But that wasn't true, was it? There were people like Janet and Mike and Simon and Megan – people who liked her and made her happy. And there were people who wanted to buy flowers from her display; people who were willing to pay money for something she had thought up! That was worth coming out of hiding for, wasn't it?

I'll try, Mum, she said in her head. *Maybe it's time to go back to being the Kate I was before. Maybe it's time to try being happy again.*

Chapter 17

Rudbeckia

'You look different,' Simon said in a puzzled voice.

Kate touched her neck self-consciously. 'I tied my hair back.'

He raised his eyebrows. 'Oh, is that it? I haven't seen your ears before.'

There was a sudden moment of confusion as they stared at each other. Simon reddened and turned away just as Kate did the same thing. She wanted to giggle. What a crazy thing to say! It wasn't exactly a compliment . . .

She couldn't believe it was her last day. The week seemed to have flown by. Anpa was home, and though he had agreed to sit down in the garden, Kate had caught him doing a sneaky bit of weeding more than once. Here at Tilworths, her flowers were so popular, she couldn't make them up fast enough. There were still mutterings about closure though, and Kate knew

that her flowers wouldn't be enough to save the garden
centre on their own. No one had been arrested for the
attack either. She felt so sad that everyone's hard work
was going to be for nothing – and what about Dimitri
Ballios? Surely he wasn't going to get away with it?
What about the evidence they'd found?

'Hey, Kate!' It was Libby, waving excitedly. 'You got
a minute?'

Kate flicked a rueful glance at Simon, who grinned
back. Of course Libby *would* turn up on her last day –
and Kate still hadn't asked Simon out. She wondered
if Libby was here to find out if Simon was available.
Brushing down her jeans, she headed over. 'Hi, Libby.
Have you got another list?'

'No, no, not today.' Libby's eyes were shining. 'Listen,
I've got something to tell you. We heard about the
break-in on the news. You know that guy who does
the breakfast show on Parchester FM?'

'Yes,' replied Kate, wondering what all this was
about.

'Well, you see over there? That's my mum, talking to
Janet – that's her name, isn't it? Anyway, Mum works
for this big promotions company, and she's done loads
of stuff for the radio station. And Steve – the presenter
– was telling her all about the amazing flowers he'd
bought from here, and how it would be criminal if

the centre closed because of this vandalism. And *I* said how great you'd been when I brought in her lists, and *she* said there might be something her company could do. *Anyway . . .*' Libby took a deep breath. 'She spoke to her bosses and they agreed they could do something out of their charity budget. They want to organize a massive promotional event here in a few weeks' time and they're going to supply all the marketing and advertising for free!'

Kate stared. 'That's brilliant! Do you think it will work? I mean . . .'

'Mum is the *best* at this kind of thing,' said Libby confidently. 'She says she reckons she can add fifty per cent on to their regular business as the result of an event like this. And she's got all sorts of ways they can raise their profile in the area too.'

'Oh wow!' Kate wanted to hug Libby. 'That's so nice of your mum! Janet will be – well, I don't suppose she'll believe it.' She couldn't help glancing over at Janet, deep in conversation with a tall, fair woman, her face flushed.

'We've only come in to raise the subject and set up a meeting,' Libby went on. 'But I just wanted to let you know. After all, if you hadn't helped me so much, I'd never have sung your praises to Mum, and neither would Steve, because the flowers thing was all your idea. And she'd never have felt she had to do something to help and taken it to her bosses, and – basically, it's all down to you!' She grinned. 'See you soon!'

'It's my last day,' Kate told her, suddenly feeling her heart sink. She really didn't want to stop working at Tilworths. It felt like a second home now.

'Oh, that's a shame.' Libby looked sympathetic. 'After all you've done here! But you'll have to come along to the event anyway.' She beamed. 'You might have single-handedly saved Tilworths!'

♥

Janet came to find Kate a little while later and swept her into a hug. 'Thank you,' she whispered. 'You've been our lucky charm this summer – you with your clever ideas for *Flowers Say It All* and your friend.'

'Libby's not exactly a friend,' Kate felt compelled to say, but she couldn't help the warm feeling that came with being hugged and praised.

'You too, Simon.' Janet broke off to hug him too. He looked embarrassed but pleased.

'Janet,' said Kate impulsively, 'why did you give Simon the job when his uncle was trying to buy this place?'

Both Simon and Janet looked taken aback, and

Simon frowned fiercely at Kate, as if to say, *What are you doing? Do you want to ruin our last day?*

'Well,' said Janet, 'because we thought he'd be a good worker.'

'But did you know he was related to Dimitri Ballios?' persisted Kate.

'Yes, of course we did. We spoke to Simon's father when his application came in.'

Simon's jaw dropped. 'You spoke to my dad?'

'Yes, on the phone. Didn't he tell you?' Janet was surprised. 'Well, there wasn't much in it. Your dad explained about the family disagreement, and how you didn't really have anything to do with your uncle at the moment. So we thought it would be fine having you here.' She pulled a face. 'If anything, we had sort of hoped that maybe you working here would have a good effect on your uncle – that maybe he would see how much you liked it and stop pressuring us.' She laughed. 'It was silly, I know, and it didn't work anyway.'

'I had no idea,' said Simon, still looking astonished.

'Well, it doesn't matter,' said Janet. Her gaze sharpened suddenly. 'Did you think – hang on . . . did you think we would treat you differently because of your uncle?'

Simon looked at the ground.

'Something like that,' said Kate.

Janet hugged Simon again. 'Don't be daft, we've loved having you here. Both of you. In fact, Mike and I have been talking—'

'Janet!' It was Mike, hurrying over. 'Janet, you've got to come with me. DS Kemmitt's here. She's got some news. She says Simon and Kate are to come too.'

'Really?' Janet's eyebrows climbed into her fringe. 'We'd better go then.'

Kate and Simon exchanged excited glances. Were they finally about to hear what had become of the Tilworths file they stole?

Detective Sergeant Kemmitt was looking very pleased with herself. 'Is there somewhere private we can talk?'

They all went through to the tiny staff room. Kate squashed into a corner whilst Simon perched on the arm of a chair next to her. She was hyper aware of his leg pressing against hers and it brought back a vivid memory of sitting next to him on the bus. She tried to concentrate.

DS Kemmitt nodded to Kate and Simon. 'It's good that you two are here because the news I have concerns you as well.' She turned to Janet and Mike. 'We've made an arrest this morning.'

Janet gasped.

DS Kemmitt nodded. 'And it's a man called Dimitri Ballios. The man who wanted to buy your land – Anatoli's uncle.'

Everyone looked at Simon, who had gone pale.

'But we wouldn't have caught him if it hadn't been for Anatoli himself,' DS Kemmitt went on. 'His and Kate's detective work gave us vital evidence.'

'Their what?' Janet asked, astonished.

DS Kemmitt explained how the two of them had gone to Dimitri's office and discovered the file on Tilworths. 'The file contained evidence linking Mr Ballios to the break-in and to all the other acts of vandalism, along with his plans to gradually lower his offer until you had no choice but to accept it. Of course, technically, taking the file amounts to theft,' she said, breaking off to look sternly at Simon and Kate. 'Which is also a prosecutable offence.'

Kate gulped.

'However,' went on DS Kemmitt, 'it seems unlikely that Mr Ballios will want to prosecute them now. We presented him with the evidence this morning and he admitted everything.'

'Just like that?' asked Mike in disbelief.

DS Kemmitt nodded. 'I think actually it was a relief in a way. I'm afraid he's in severe financial trouble.'

'Uncle Dimitri?' Simon was shocked. 'But he has loads of money.'

DS Kemmitt shook her head. 'Not any more. Some of the houses he developed have serious faults, and the tenants are bringing lawsuits against him. It seems he's been borrowing money from some dubious lenders. He's over his head in debt.'

So that was why he kept on with the court case against Simon's grandmother's will! thought Kate. *He was desperately hoping he would win and receive a share of her money – enough to get him out of trouble anyway.* She caught Simon's eye and knew he was thinking the same thing.

'Then why would he try to buy our land?' asked Janet, bewildered. 'If he didn't have any money?'

'My guess is he was going to try to raise the capital against future gains,' said DS Kemmitt. 'If he could get the land for half of what it's worth, he could make a profit immediately. And when you turned down his initial offer, he got desperate and tried to intimidate you into selling up.'

'It nearly worked,' commented Mike. He reached over to take Janet's hand.

'I can't believe it,' said Janet, shaking her head. 'All of our problems – all of it his fault!'

'Don't worry,' DS Kemmitt reassured her, 'he'll be

facing several charges. He won't be causing you any more trouble.'

'What about his receptionist?' asked Kate suddenly. Julie had been nice to her; she felt bad that they'd betrayed her.

'She may well be facing charges too,' DS Kemmitt said. 'She knew more than she was letting on, but she kept quiet because she didn't want to lose her job.'

Ballet is expensive, thought Kate with regret, wondering if Julie's daughters would have to stop lessons because she'd lost her job. The file had been in Julie's cabinet, so she must have known, but still Kate couldn't help feeling sorry for her.

'Well,' said Mike, 'this is turning out to be the best morning we've had in a long time!'

'We had some other good news,' Janet told the detective. 'A local company is going to do some promotional events for us to bring in more business.'

DS Kemmitt smiled. 'That's great. I must say, I'm delighted we've been able to wrap up the case. And it's thanks to these two, really – though I don't expect them to make a habit of theft.' She fixed them with a steely glare.

'Of course not,' said Kate hastily. She looked down at Simon. His face was blank and suddenly she was anxious for him. How was he feeling? After all, Dimitri was his uncle – he was *family*. She put a hand on his shoulder. 'You OK?'

He didn't seem to hear her.

DS Kemmitt was telling Janet and Mike that the case wouldn't come to court for several months and that Mr Ballios would likely be released on bail. Kate barely listened; she was worrying about Simon. When the DS finally left, Janet and Mike went out with her.

Kate squeezed out of the uncomfortable corner and sat down in a chair opposite Simon. His hands were clutched together so tightly his knuckles were white.

'Are you OK?' she asked, and then wanted to kick herself. Of *course* he wasn't OK! What a dumb thing to say! 'Sorry, I mean . . . um.'

'In *debt*,' said Simon, his eyes still glaring at nothing. 'No money! I can't believe it.'

'Yeah.'

'The will . . . my grandma . . . cutting him out because he had all that money – and now he has nothing.'

Kate hesitated. 'Do you feel sorry for him?'

'For *him*?' He turned blazing eyes on her and she flinched. 'Of course not! He's squandered it all! Trampled on people – look what he did here!'

'Then . . .'

'You know, I didn't want to believe it,' Simon went on. 'Even when we had the file, it was like some kind

of dream. We were playing detectives, but I kept
expecting to find out we were wrong. He's my *uncle*.'

'I know.'

'But I don't feel sorry for *him*. It's my cousins. He's
got three children. I haven't seen them for ages, but we
used to play together all the time when we were little.
One big Greek family, you know. Me and my brothers
and sister got on really well with them.' He looked
down at his hands. 'I just keep thinking what if that
was my dad? Spending all the money and then getting
arrested. What are they going to do now?'

Kate reached out to put her hands on his. 'It's not
your fault.'

'Yeah, but if it hadn't been for us taking the file . . .
he'd never have been caught, would he?'

'Are you saying you wish he *hadn't* been caught?'

'No, of course not. Well – no. But I wish it hadn't
been him.'

'Maybe you could get back in touch with them?'
suggested Kate tentatively. 'I mean, I know it's been
a big family argument, but it's not between you and
your cousins, is it? Why don't you, I don't know, email
them or something?'

Simon thought for a moment. 'Yeah. I guess maybe
I could. Like you say, it's not really our problem. But I
don't want to upset my dad.'

The two of them sat in silence for a while. 'Families, eh?' said Simon eventually.

Kate gave a small smile. 'Totally.' His hands felt cold under hers, and she squeezed them more tightly.

He looked up and made an attempt at a smile. 'Still, I guess we did a good job, right? I mean, we brought him to justice or whatever they call it. And the attacks and the break-ins will all stop now, and Janet and Mike don't have to sell up for a stupid price.'

'Yeah.' Kate smiled back. 'We did the right thing.'

'Proper heroes.'

'Yeah . . .' His face was only inches away. *Now!* the voice thundered in her head. *Now is the perfect time! Tell him how you feel! Tell him!*

'We should probably get back to work.' Simon sat back, pulling his hands away.

Kate felt absurdly disappointed. She had almost managed to say it . . . 'OK.' *You missed your chance again*, she told herself sadly as she followed Simon out of the room. *And it's the last day. That's it. You've blown it.*

Chapter 18

Celandine

It was late afternoon, and Kate and Simon were re-stacking the cardboard boxes by the till, which were used by customers to carry home their plants. Kate felt utterly miserable. Why hadn't she seized the moment, as Anpa had told her to? How could she have blown all the chances she'd been given to tell Simon she'd like to see him again? And now it was the very last day at Tilworths and she wouldn't get any more chances. It was all she could do to stop herself bursting into tears right there and then.

'Kate!'

Kate swung round just before a small ball of energy barrelled into her. It was Owen, Megan's five-year-old brother. 'Oof!'

'Who's this?' Simon asked, amused.

'This is Owen,' Kate said, as Owen clung to her legs, grinning at Simon. *Oh no, Megan and her family must be here to buy the hose today! Why couldn't they have come yesterday?*

'We're going to buy a hose,' Owen told Simon.

'That's nice.'

'Hey.' Megan, her auburn hair set off perfectly by her summer tan, hurried into the centre. 'Owen, you mustn't run off like that! Mum's going mad!' She smiled at Kate. 'Hello, stranger. I like the apron.'

Megan's mum and dad followed her in. 'Hello, Kate. Megan says it's your last day today, is that right?'

'Yes.'

'You must be Simon,' Megan said, smiling even more broadly. 'I've heard so much about you.'

Simon looked taken aback. 'Oh – have you?'

'Oh *yes*,' went on Megan, ignoring Kate's blushes, 'Kate's always talking about you.'

'Really?' He glanced at her.

'Is Simon your boyfriend?' asked Owen bluntly.

Fortunately, Kate was saved from having to answer by the arrival of two more people. 'Anpa! Dad! What are you doing here?'

'Oh, that's nice, that is,' said Anpa, with a twinkle in his eye. He walked more slowly than usual but otherwise he looked well. 'Can't a man come and visit his granddaughter?'

'Dad, aren't you supposed to be at work?'

Nick looked very smug. 'Booked the day off. Janet and Mike asked us to come in.'

'Really? Kate turned to gaze across the shop. 'Why?'

'Where's the hose?' asked Owen. 'Can I have a windmill?'

Kate felt as though she were suddenly swept up in a whirlwind. There were people everywhere! Carol came bustling over. 'Why don't you all go outside? The sun's out, you could show everyone your flower display, Kate.'

Kate caught Simon's eye. He was looking as baffled as she was. What was going on? They began to make their way through the shop, though Megan's mum Nicola had to detach Owen from almost every item on the way. 'No, you can't have that. No, Owen. *No*.'

Anpa leaned past Kate to shake Simon's hand. 'Hello, young man. You must be Simon. I'm glad Kate's found a keen fellow gardener, working here.'

A keen fellow gardener? Kate briefly closed her eyes in embarrassment. If her family and friends were going to say cringeworthy things to the boy she liked, she wished they'd stayed away! She avoided her father's interested gaze. 'This way,' she said hurriedly.

They reached the outside area and Kate's dad found a bench for Anpa to sit down. A couple of metres to their right was the *Flowers Say It All* display, and Kate was just about to point it out to Anpa when there was another shout from the shop. 'Anatoli!' Everyone turned to see two more people coming along behind.

'Mum!' said Simon in surprise. 'Althea – I didn't know you were coming in.'

So this was Simon's mother and sister! Kate stared in frank curiosity at the dark-haired, dark-eyed girl who was the spitting image of her older brother. Simon's mother also had the same dark eyes and hair, though her face was rounder than her children's.

'Sorry your father couldn't make it,' she said to Simon. In a low voice, she added, 'He's – er – he's gone down to the police station.'

'Oh.'

'There's something – well, your uncle Dimitri . . .'

'We know,' Simon said, glancing at Kate. 'The police came to tell us. Mum, this is Kate. You know, I – er – told you about her.'

He's talked to his mum about me? Kate felt her stomach flip. She'd have given anything to know what he'd said!

The woman reached out a graceful hand. 'It's lovely to meet you,' she said.

Kate then felt she needed to introduce them to everyone else as well. By the time she'd got through everyone, Janet and Mike had appeared, along with a smiling Polly.

'Surprise!' said Janet. She was holding a small cake. Beside her, Mike shushed everyone.

'Kate and Simon have been with us for the summer,' he began.

Oh no! thought Kate. *I didn't realize they would do speeches and everything!* She felt her face start to flame with embarrassment.

'And they've really become part of the team,' Mike went on. 'They have worked extremely hard and, between them, they may just have saved Tilworths from going under.' His eyes met Kate's before moving to Simon, and his gaze said it all.

Kate felt like she wanted to cry. They had all been so lovely to her!

'Anyway,' said Janet, 'we haven't got a lot to give you, but Polly made a cake and Carol iced it for us.' She held it out so they could see the green THANK YOU piped across the middle, and the tiny blue forget-me-nots that decorated the sides. 'We chose forget-me-nots because we don't want you to forget us,' she said with a smile. 'You've taught us a lot about the language of flowers, Kate.'

'That's beautiful,' said Megan's mum, and there was a murmur of agreement.

Janet hesitated. 'We're saying thank you and good bye, but actually Mike and I have something to ask the two of you – and your families.' She looked around. 'Our daughter Louise has decided to go travelling for her gap year, and we'd thought she would be joining us at work. So we'd like to ask Kate and Simon to carry on working here on Saturdays. Assuming you all agree, of course.'

The world spun slightly. Kate wasn't sure she could take any more surprises today! 'I'd love to!' she said immediately, and everyone laughed.

'Me too,' agreed Simon, smiling. 'Besides, I can't leave Kate to do her flower displays on her own. Her handwriting is awful.'

Kate's father laughed. 'You're not wrong there. She gets it from me, I'm afraid.' He grinned at her.

Simon's mum nodded. 'I don't see why you shouldn't carry on working here, *kamari-mou*. As long as your father doesn't mind.'

Anpa was frowning. 'I'm not sure it's a good idea. Kate's got school work to do, you know.'

'Oh, Anpa, please . . .' Then she saw he was smiling.

'Just pulling your leg, love. I think it's a great idea.'

Kate thought she might explode with happiness. What an amazing day this was turning out to be!

And best of all, she'd still be seeing Simon every week! Megan grinned at her, and Kate knew she was thinking the same thing.

'Right,' said Janet, 'that's sorted then! Mike and I have got to get back to work, I'm afraid, but we're going to leave you with the cake. Don't worry about doing any more jobs. Just make sure you come to say goodbye at the end – and we'll see you next Saturday!'

'Cake!' cried Owen enthusiastically.

Within minutes, they were all munching happily on slices of the creamy confection. 'Delicious,' said Anpa, getting icing on his nose. 'And this display of yours is lovely, Kate.' He pointed to a small shrub. 'That's a very late flowering gardenia. What does the label say?'

'*Happiness*,' read Nick.

'I like that,' said Anpa, approvingly. 'We should have one of those in our garden.'

'But Anpa, you don't like flowers,' said Kate, smiling. 'You can't eat them.'

He wagged his finger. 'Don't you quote my own words back at me, young lady. I know what I'm talking about. We need a bit of happiness in our garden.'

'We'll have to take it with us when we move,' said Nick hesitantly, picking up the gardenia pot. ' I – um,

I put the house on the market this morning. I hope that's all right with the two of you.'

Kate smiled. 'Of course it is.'

Anpa nodded. 'That can be the first plant to go in the new garden, then. Excellent. Happiness it is.' He grinned at Kate.

Megan's mum had been looking at the display too. 'These are beautiful. What a wonderful idea. You're so talented, Kate.'

'Oh, no, I'm not really—'

'Yes, you are,' Simon interrupted, to her surprise. Megan trod hard on her foot and gave her a meaningful look.

'It's nearly time to go,' Nick said, looking at his watch. 'Do you want to go and get your things, Kate? We'll wait here for you.'

'Don't hurry,' Anpa said, his eyes gleaming as he gazed across the shelves. 'I want a little look round anyway.'

'Don't even think about it,' Nick told him. 'You point to what you'd like to see and I'll bring it over.'

'That's no good,' grumbled Anpa. 'I'm not an invalid any more, you know.'

Nick grinned, and then a thought struck him. 'Oh, Kate, by the way, we stopped at a travel agent's on the way here and picked up some brochures. Thought you might like to choose where we go on holiday next year.'

'Wow.' Kate couldn't believe her ears. 'I'd love to!'

Simon followed Kate into the shop and through to the staff area. 'What was your dad saying about a holiday?'

'We haven't been anywhere since Mum died,' Kate explained. 'Dad always said he was too busy at work.'

'And he's not now?'

'It's like me and my dad are starting again.' She shook her head, marvelling. 'Anpa's heart attack was so scary and I thought he was going to die. But it's weird the difference it's made to us all. My dad had some stuff he didn't want to talk about, but it's getting better now. And he's not spending so much time at work either.'

'That's good.' Simon sighed. 'I hope things will be OK for us too. I'm guessing my dad will put up bail for Uncle Dimitri.'

'But I thought they hated each other.'

'They're still brothers though, aren't they? I can't imagine Dad abandoning him, no matter what he's done.' He suddenly looked at her. 'It's been a bit of a crazy summer, hasn't it?'

'Totally.'

'I've got something for you.' He turned and pushed open the fire door to the little yard.

'For me?' She was intrigued but a little alarmed. *I didn't get anything for him!*

Simon pointed. 'There.'

It was a ceramic pot, bright blue, housing a small feathery plant. 'Is that an acacia?' asked Kate, puzzled.

'Yes. It's taken me ages to find one. It's not in flower yet, but it'll be yellow.'

'Yellow acacia?' She picked up the pot. 'There's no label.'

'No. I – uh, I didn't do one.' Was he *blushing*?

'Acacia . . . acacia . . .' Kate shook her head. 'It's no good, I can't remember – what does it mean?'

'Oh – I'm sure you can look it up.' Simon was *definitely* blushing now.

Kate felt the heat rise in her own cheeks. What on earth did yellow acacia mean in the language of flowers? Was it . . . was it something romantic? 'Can't you tell me?'

He shook his head. 'No, you – you find out what it is and then let me know.'

'Let you know what?'

'Oh, never mind. You've got my number anyway.'

Kate was burning to know what the flower meant.

Suddenly she remembered – she had *The Ultimate Language of Flowers* in her bag! 'Hang on a minute,' she said, putting the pot down. 'I've got the book with me now.'

'No!' Simon stepped forward quickly and put his hand on her arm. 'No, don't – please. It's . . . well, you'll see when you read it. But *please* don't look now.'

'All right.' She looked at him. How could it have taken her so long to realize how completely gorgeous he was? Those chocolate-brown eyes and the way he looked at her . . .

Simon smiled. 'You've gone kind of pink.'

'So have you,' she whispered.

'You look pretty.'

Before she could even take this in, he leaned forward to kiss her on the cheek. It was gentle, fleeting – only lasting a second or two. But the place his lips touched tingled and fizzed like sunburn. And then, his face reddening as much as hers, he turned and fled, calling out, 'Let me know!' over his shoulder.

Hurriedly, she scrabbled in her bag for the book. Fingers shaking, she turned the pages. Was it under 'yellow' or 'acacia'? There – there it was!

Kate stood still as she read the meaning. A tingling swept through her. *Wow! Can he really mean it?* She looked at the plant again. Who would have thought that one summer could change everything?

Smiling, she closed the book. She would let him know, of course – her fingers were itching to text him right now, but she forced herself not to. She needed to let it sink in; to remind herself that she'd been through some bad times; but it was time.

Time to be happy again.

♥

The Language of Flowers –
some common meanings*

Amethyst – admiration
Bluebell – constancy, fidelity
Cactus – warmth
Campanula – gratitude
Carnation (red, pink or white) – pure love
Celandine – joys to come
Chrysanthemum – cheerfulness
Crocosmia – bravery, valour
Daffodil – regard
Daisy – innocence
Fig – argument, quarrelsome
Forget-me-not – true love, remember me
Freesia – sweetness
Garden marigold – uneasiness
Geranium – comfort
Gloxinia – proud of spirit
Heather – solitude
Ivy – fidelity, friendship, ties
Judas tree – betrayal

Larch – audacity, boldness
Lilac – first emotions of affection
Lily – purity, elegance, beauty
Lily of the valley – return of happiness
Mandrake – horror
Mistletoe – I will overcome all difficulties
Osier – honesty, frankness
Peppermint – warmth of feeling
Periwinkle – memories of friendship
Poppy – sleep, dreaming
Primrose – youth
Rose – love
Rosemary – remembrance
Rudbeckia – justice
Scotch thistle – retaliation
Tulip – fame
Vervain – enchantment
Violet – faithfulness
Wallflower – stick together through tough times
White clover – think of me

And, of course . . .
Yellow acacia – secret love

*with thanks to *Kate Greenaway's Language of Flowers*
and *The Ultimate Language of Flowers* by Rob Cassy.

You can meet some of the Sweet Heart girls again
in the brand-new book

Ice
Dreams

Available soon

Read on to find out who . . .

'So,' said Libby, 'how did it go? Did you put your foot down?'

Tania smiled ruefully. 'Yes. And then Brock stamped on it.'

Libby's eyes opened wide. 'No! He really stamped on your foot? With a *skate*? Oh my God!'

Tania laughed. 'You idiot, Lib. Of course he didn't really stamp on my foot. You are so literal.'

'Thank God!' Libby wiped imaginary sweat from her brow. 'For a minute there I was imagining your foot sliced in half.'

'Ew.'

'Well, exactly. So what happened then?' Libby threw her bag onto the floor next to the table and pulled a squashed sandwich out of her pocket. 'Oh no, Mum made me cheese salad again. I told her not to put tomatoes in, they just make everything else soggy.'

'You should make your own lunch then,' said Tania primly, producing a small lunchbox.

'You can talk! When have you ever made your own packed lunch?' commented Libby. 'Your mum still makes yours too.'

'Only because I get up so early to go to the rink,' said Tania. 'She says if I made my own lunch in the mornings we'd never get there for six a.m.'

Libby lost interest in Tania's mum. 'Never mind that, what about the training? What about . . .' she lowered her voice, '*Zac*?'

Tania bit into her sandwich and thought back to the previous afternoon. 'It didn't start very well. I was a bit mad, to tell you the truth. Maybe I went a bit over the top.'

'You? Never,' said Libby loyally, and then ruined the effect by snorting with laughter. 'I can't think of a single time you've ever gone over the top before . . . oh wait, except that time you found out Mrs Lafayette had timetabled your French Oral at the same time as your last NISA test . . . and then the time your skates weren't ready when they said they would be and you just went mad because you wanted to practise that evening . . . and then there were the other fifty-three times . . .'

'*Anyway*,' went on Tania, ignoring Libby's malicious

giggle, 'we only did a bit of practice but it was all right. Not amazing, but not as bad as I thought it was going to be.' She hesitated. 'Do I really go over the top that much?'

'Yes,' said Libby affectionately, 'but I still like you. Can't think why.'

Tania pulled a face. 'I can't think why either.'

Libby laughed. 'Oh, Tania! You are so serious sometimes! Maybe that's why we make such good friends. You're too serious and I'm not serious enough!'

'We are complete opposites, aren't we?' asked Tania with a rueful smile.

'Just as well too,' said Libby, picking slices of tomato out of her sandwich and piling them on the table. 'I couldn't be friends with someone exactly like me. I mean, what would we talk about? Except boys, of course.'

Tania watched her friend make a pile of soggy tomatoes. 'That's disgusting, Lib.'

'Speaking of *boys*,' went on Libby, 'what's he like? Zac.'

'He's all right. Not as rude as I thought.'

'Aha!' Libby waggled her eyebrows. 'I knew it! Romance blossoms on the ice.'

Tania shook her head in amusement. 'You have

such a one-track mind. It's not like that at all. He's not even my type. He's far too laid-back for me. I'm really driven; ambitious. He's not like that at all.'

'Uh-huh.'

'What's that supposed to mean?'

'What colour are his eyes?' asked Libby.

'Hazel,' said Tania automatically.

'HA!'

'What?'

Libby leaned forward and waved a slice of tomato at her friend. 'You've noticed his eyes! That can mean only one thing . . .'

'They're either side of his nose?' suggested Tania.

'You fancy him!' announced Libby dramatically.

'I do not!' said Tania. 'Lib, honestly, it's just skating. It's only for a couple of months; just till the show. That's all.'

'Hmm,' said Libby. 'That's what *you* say.'

Tania laughed. 'Even if I did feel like that, Zac wouldn't look at me twice. We're from different worlds. Besides, he knows singles is my career. He's just in it for the fun. He's so laid-back, he'll probably forget all about practice today anyway.'

Libby made a face. 'Say what you like,' she said loftily, the effect slightly spoilt by the dab of mayonnaise on her nose. 'This is the beginning of a beautiful relationship. I just know it.'

♥